DANGER LEVEL 4

A Kori Briggs Adventure

A.P. Rawls

Upper West Side Press, LLC

Danger Level 4

A Kori Briggs Adventure

A.P. Rawls

FIRST PRINTING

ISBN: 978-1-7372613-6-0

eBook ISBN: 978-1-7372613-7-7

Large Print Edition: 978-1-7372613-8-4

Library of Congress Control Number: 2022904827

UWS

Upper West Side Press, LLC

**The Kori Briggs series of adventure spy novels
by A.P. Rawls:**

The Dark Tetrad

In this action-packed Kori Briggs debut novel, Kori is on the trail of a madman who has managed to steal a hundred pounds of uranium and, with the help of an equally twisted Russian scientist, is intent on detonating a nuclear bomb somewhere in the world. But when and where? Come along with Kori on this vicarious thrill ride as she follows clues from Washington, DC to New York City, Russia, Israel, and finally, Paris, the "City of Lights."

We'll Quit When We're Dead

Everyone's favorite secret agent is once again globetrotting around the world to save the day. This time she's investigating a real and imminent threat from a foreign power, a potential terrorist act on American soil so extensive that its successful deployment could well result in World War III. Follow Kori from San Francisco to Vancouver to Istanbul as she races against time to prevent a cataclysmic collision with destiny.

Danger Level 4

In this third book of the A.P. Rawls series of Kori Briggs suspense spy thrillers, Kori has landed in the middle of a South American revolution. Super-secret spy organization Rampart has intelligence that a dictator with weapons of mass destruction is about to be overthrown. But who are the revolutionaries, and are they any less dangerous? The stability of the Western Hemisphere is at stake. Follow Kori through the jungles, hills, and perilous streets of a nation on the brink of war with itself!

The Prince is Missing!

In this fourth book of the series, Kori has been tasked with the assignment of finding England's missing Prince Grayson! All signs point to a kidnapping at the hands of an American ex-con, but Kori knows there's much more to the story. Follow her and her trusty Russian sidekick Anya Kovalev as they scour the grand city of London for clues to the prince's disappearance!

Get a free gift when you register for updates at https://koribriggs.com/connect/

UWS
Upper West Side Press, LLC

1

—·—

Whenever Kori Briggs went on vacation, and it wasn't very often, she liked to go to places that had remained more or less undiscovered by the masses. She hated crowds and despised standing in lines. In Italy, the most popular tourist destinations are, in order, Rome, Florence, and Venice, followed by the Amalfi Coast and the Tuscany region.

Which is why Kori Briggs was in Mantua.

Mantua—or Mantova to the locals as Venezia is to Venice—is located in Northern Italy and referred to by those in the know as the Italian capital of culture. A World Heritage site, the city of roughly fifty thousand, passed over by most travelers, is home to museums, beautiful medieval and Renaissance architecture, magnificent cathedrals, narrow cobbled streets that lead to open piazzas and courtyards, theaters with live opera, and friendly people, all of it resting on a lake, or, more accurately, three adjoining lakes that surround the old part of the city. And—no small thing as far as Kori was concerned—a plethora of fine eating establishments. Mantua, in fact, has been named

European Capital of Gastronomy. This was Kori's kind of place.

At Trattoria al Gallo, a charming little spot that served a grilled rib of beef—*costata di manzo ai ferri*—Kori was sampling some of the fine dining that the city had to offer, washing it down with a bottle of Fontodi red 2016, a full-bodied wine that was just right for bringing out the rich flavors of the dish. At the moment, the stresses and strains of her unique occupation were out of sight and out of mind.

The day had been a whirlwind of sightseeing. From her suite at Valenti-Gonzaga Palace, a historic and luxurious hotel, Kori had made her way to the Ducale Palace, home of royalty since the fourteenth century; the Piazza Broletto, a large square surrounded by medieval buildings; and the beautiful Basilica of Sant'Andrea; all of which doubled as both architectural masterpieces and art museums, with sculptures and medieval frescoes and tapestries and early Renaissance paintings. Then, having experienced sufficient culture for the day, she had taken in the shops, including a high-end clothing boutique where she picked up a Loretta Camponi blouse and a pair of Christian Louboutin pumps.

It had been a wonderful day.

Tomorrow there would be more of the same. Kori already had her breakfast spot picked out, a café down the street that served frittatas, ricotta pancakes, brioche, and cappuccinos. After that, she figured she would rent a car and see the countryside. Verona was a one-hour drive north through farmland and vineyards. She had no plan for when she got to Verona and that's the way she wanted it. She'd scope it out and do whatever appealed to her in the moment. It was going to be another magical day. Life was good.

And then . . .

Midway into the cannoli she was having for dessert, her phone rang. She looked at the screen and winced. *Damn*, she thought. The one call she had to take. The one call she could never ignore. Being always accessible was practically part of the oath.

She put the phone up to her ear. "Briggs here."

"Hi, Briggs. How's Italy?" One thing Kori knew about Rampart Director Richard Eaglethorpe was that he would never think of calling his top agent during a vacation unless it was something serious. Another thing she knew was that, even though he asked, he didn't really care about her trip to Italy. Not at that moment, anyway. There was business at hand.

"Well, it's great, Chief," Kori replied, "but something tells me it's coming to a close."

"Good intuition as always, Agent Briggs. One of the many things that separate you from the rest. Of course, there are so *many* things."

"Yep. That's how I also know that this flattery is leading someplace."

"Right again. Yeah, Briggs, sorry about this. I'm afraid duty calls."

"Okay, what's the scoop?"

"Are you familiar with Miranda?"

"Miranda? The girl that works in the coffee shop in our building? Short, with that pixie haircut?"

"No, no, no. The country."

"Oh, *that* Miranda. Well, let's see. South America. Bordered by Brazil and Uruguay. Population around 25 million, I believe. Capital city San Benito. Chief export is oil. It's a dictatorship, led by Presidente Alonso Estrada. Lots of drugs and crime, as I recall. Not exactly a vacation destination for the fam."

"That's the place."

"So what's going on in Miranda, Chief?"

"That's what we need to find out. There have been a lot of rumblings. Our man Vidal in Brazil just called me. He's laid up at his home in Rio de Janeiro recovering from a gunshot wound. I don't know all the details. Apparently, on a reconnaissance mission to Miranda, he was caught in the crossfire between some governmental police and a group of dissidents in the hills outside San Benito."

"There are dissidents?"

"There sure are. Evidently, a whole guerrilla movement is underway. Vidal managed to get away and get treated. Now he's back at his home recovering. But he assures me that the makings of a bona fide revolution are brewing in Miranda."

"Wow. Well, is Vidal okay?"

"He'll be fine. Hit him in the leg. Can't walk very well just now, but in a few weeks, he should be as right as rain."

"Well, Chief, from what I know about Presidente Estrada, a revolution would be a good thing, wouldn't it? I mean, he's supposedly pretty cutthroat."

"Well, you'd think so, but for right now, the efforts of these people are creating a lot of pushback by the government. They've restarted the purges. Hundreds are being rounded up, maybe thousands. It's as bad now as it's ever been, going back to the *Sangrado*."

"Yes, 'The bleeding.' Not a great time for Miranda."

"Yeah, you could say that. Over a two-month period, Estrada had his *Policia Nacional* round up tens of thousands of people whom he deemed a threat to his regime. Some sent to prison camps, some simply executed."

"I remember. The national police is a scary group, Chief."

"We need to get a handle on what's going on down there, Kori. This could have an impact on the whole region. Estrada has created a pretty formidable army and it would be a mess if the problems of Miranda spilled over to its neighbors. The main danger, of course, is Estrada's nuclear weapons program."

"How advanced is it?"

"Nobody really knows. But if a power-hungry, paranoid guy like Estrada believes he's being ousted, he might not be so reluctant to use what he's got, even if it's nuclear and even if it's rudimentary. South America is a political minefield right now as it is. This could further destabilize things. The whole continent is at stake, depending on how serious this is."

"What's the official US position on Miranda?"

"You know our government. Priority one is to keep the hemisphere safe from communism. Whatever the cost. Priority two is stability. And so the CIA loves guys like

Estrada, so long as they can keep order. Estrada has maintained good relations with the US and kept the oil flowing northward, which naturally is another major priority. And he's eschewed involvement from the Russians and Chinese, even though both have made multiple overtures."

"And what's our position, Chief?"

"Agent Briggs, you know Rampart stays apolitical. Our independent little intelligence organization is only interested in the safety and well-being of the nation's citizens."

"Sure, Chief. That's our official stance, or would be if anybody knew about us. But you're the boss. What do *you* think?"

"I'm not paid to think, Kori. Just to act. As are you. However, since you asked, and since I assume you'll keep asking until I answer—"

"You know me well, Chief."

"—my completely unofficial position is that Estrada is a murdering son of a bitch."

"So his administration should be overthrown."

"I didn't say that, Briggs. What does his administration get replaced with? Another murdering son of a bitch? This is the problem with revolutions. To paraphrase a great man, they're like a box of chocolates. You never know what you're going to get."

"I think the great man was quoting his mother, Chief, but I see what you mean. Nobody wants to see bad go to worse."

"Which is why we need you to nose around down there. Find out what's going on. Touch base with the rebel faction. Poke around the capital; see if you can get someone in the government to talk to you. Feel out both sides. And it wouldn't hurt to do a little reconnaissance of our CIA presence down there. Find out what they know and what kind of intel they're sending back to Washington. I hate being at cross-purposes with those guys, but we need to know if they're going to make the situation better or worse. If they're planning on doing anything at all, that is."

"Right, Chief. I understand."

"Cooper has booked you on a flight first thing in the morning to Rio to meet with Agent Vidal. He'll tell you what he knows and then you can cross the border into Miranda. We'll prepare all the documentation you'll need."

"Okay. I'll be on that flight."

"Great. Oh, and sorry about your vacation."

"It's okay, Chief. A person can only take so much fun and relaxation."

2

—— • ——

Kori got to take that drive to Verona, after all. Unfortunately, it was only so that she could get to Verona International Airport. And her plane left early, meaning she didn't have time for breakfast at that café down the street. By sunrise, she had put Mantua and her wonderful Italian vacation in her rearview mirror.

Her KLM Airlines flight took her first to Amsterdam, a five-hour flight that landed early, stretching her turnaround time for her Rio flight to three hours at Schiphol Airport. She toyed with the idea of taking a cab into the city. As much as she had traveled throughout Europe, she'd never been to Amsterdam. When would she get another chance? But she thought better of it. The flight to Rio was the only one leaving Schiphol that day and she couldn't imagine missing it and having to explain to Eaglethorpe why she hadn't arrived in Rio when she was supposed to. *Sorry, Chief, I lost track of time in the Van Gogh museum.* Instead, Kori found an airport restaurant that served Dutch cuisine and Grolsch beer. *This'll have to do*, she thought, feasting on a plate of *bit-*

terballen—deep-fried, beef-based balls with a breadcrumb coating. Adding a plate of Gouda cheese and two Grolsch beers to the meal gave her the sustenance she'd need to face the twelve-hour flight to Rio. Fortunately, Cooper had booked her into business class complete with all the niceties—privacy canopy, seat that reclined to a fully flat position, extra-large entertainment screen, gourmet dinner, and complimentary adult beverages. The only way to travel.

Before boarding, she took the time to call her mother, just to check in and, more importantly, to give her mother a reason, albeit fabricated, to not worry about her daughter.

Joan Briggs, as always, was thrilled to hear from her. "Are you enjoying Italy, dear?" she asked.

"I sure am, Mom. It's a fascinating place. In fact, I've decided that I'm going to stick around for a few more days."

"You are? That's great, Kori, but will your company allow it?"

"Sure, I just called my boss. He's fine with it. There's nothing really urgent going on just now and I think he believes that I deserve the extra time off."

"You certainly do, dear. You work awfully hard. I'm sure Gladstone Conveyor can do without their East Coast VP of sales for a few more days."

"I agree, Mom."

"Well, be safe over there, Kori. You know that I worry about you when you're away."

"I know you do, Mom, and it's sweet of you. But you know me. Miss Sensible. Nothing crazy for this girl. Just a few guided tours here and there and back in my hotel room by dark. So what's new with you?"

"Well, you're not going to believe this, but I've started taking ballroom dance classes!"

"No!"

"Yep. Gwen Robbins from my book club convinced me to give it a try. I was skeptical at first, but I have to admit that I'm having a marvelous time. The mambo, the foxtrot, the cha-cha . . ."

"Mom, it sounds like you're the crazy one!"

Joan laughed and told Kori all about the class. The instructor was nice and the other students were all a lot of fun. There were even a few older, eligible bachelors in the class, Joan had to confess, giggling. One of those eligible bachelors was a charming man named Bertram who could waltz like nobody's business.

Joan talked some more and then the two said their good-byes, with Kori promising to keep in touch and Joan once again imploring her daughter to be safe.

Twelve hours, one dinner, two glasses of wine, one Scotch, a nap, and two movies later, Kori's plane touched down at Galeão International Airport in Rio de Janeiro. During the flight, Kori had also taken the time to read a short brief Cooper had emailed her on Miranda. The situation wasn't pretty. San Benito, the capital and largest city, had become the murder capital of the world. Approximately one murder every twenty-one minutes. Gangs roamed the streets. Drugs were rampant. So was *Policia*

Nacional but the sight of the government police force was hardly reassuring to the people in the barrios; the police were corrupt and most did the bidding of Presidente Alonso Estrada if one of the major drug cartels didn't buy their loyalty first. The US State Department had classified Miranda as a Level 4 travel risk. Level 1 is reasonably safe. Level 2 suggests a traveler should exercise caution. Level 3 means a traveler should reconsider her plans. The advisory for a Level 4 country is curt and straightforward: *Do not travel*. There is no Level 5.

Kori's watch, still on Mantua time, said 5:10 a.m. when she got into a taxi at the airport. Her phone displayed the local time: 1:10 a.m. She'd be meeting with Rampart agent Roberto Vidal mid-morning, so she had some time to kill. The taxi took her to the famed Copacabana Palace Hotel on Avenida Atlântica, a 1923 landmark and five-star resort where Cooper had booked her a suite overlooking the ocean.

Kori would only be in Rio for a couple of nights before making her way south to Miranda, but, as Agent Darren Cooper knew all too well, she preferred to visit a place in style. Her expense account was basically limitless. Rampart's funding was, too. The autonomous, super-secret spy organization had reaped the benefits of thwarting the nefarious plans of an ultra-wealthy terrorist. To the victors went the spoils, or at least a portion of them, about a billion dollars put into a trust account from which Rampart took a handsome monthly withdrawal. The unlimited expense account was a wonderful perk. How many jobs offered that? Then again, few jobs came with the same level of risk.

Kori checked in, found her room, and, knowing her internal clock was fouled up and sleep was not going to come easy, slipped into a hot bath first. Then she climbed into bed for a few hours of tossing and turning before waking to the Brazilian sun streaming through her hotel window. She made a cup of coffee with the room's Keurig, took a quick shower, dressed, and headed off to meet Vidal.

Besides its luxury, there was another reason for staying at the Copacabana Palace; it was only a ten-minute taxi drive to Vidal's apartment in Ipanema. Most of it was along Avenida Atlântica, giving Kori a view of not only the ocean but of the beautiful people of the city strolling along the broad sidewalk that ran between the avenue and the extensive beach. It was mid-morning, but countless beach umbrellas were already populating the sand and numerous bathers dotted the warm surf. *Another fine vacation spot,* Kori thought. *For another time, perhaps.*

Roberto Vidal was a native Brazilian although he had grown up not in the city of Rio de Janeiro, but about eighty-five miles west in Volta Redonda. His father worked in the steel mill there and the mill was a point of pride for the locals. It had opened in 1946, the first steel mill in all of South America. Today, the Presidente Vargas Steelworks is one of the largest in the world. But Roberto didn't want to work in the steel mill and, against his father's wishes, left home after high school for a university degree. His father understood the desire for a better education. What he didn't understand was Roberto's desire to obtain it in the United States. But Roberto wanted to see something of the world, and especially the US, a land that seemed to young Roberto as though it had everything a young man could ever want.

He applied to the University of Miami because he wanted to go north, but not too far north. He was accepted as an international student and earned a degree in criminology, eventually acquiring not just a diploma, but American citizenship. Then he stayed in Miami, enrolling in the Miami police academy, graduating with honors, and working for a couple of years for the Miami PD, mostly in the Little Havana section where he earned a medal for heroism and a meritorious service award. His father back in Volta Redonda was proud of him and his move to the US was forgiven. Roberto made detective in short order, but setting his sights higher, he applied to be a special agent with the FBI, a grueling process that took him over a year and a half to complete. Once accepted, he soared through his training with distinction, and in his first full year of duty, he discovered and almost single-handedly stopped a domestic terrorist cell in Tampa from carrying out a cyberattack on the Department of Defense.

That's when he got the attention of Rampart. Director Eaglethorpe recruited him. Rampart needed an agent in South America. Vidal's father had become ill and Roberto had been thinking of returning to Brazil anyway. The timing was right. So was the money. Vidal gave a story to the FBI that his family needed him back in Volta Redonda, where he was going to head up the security department of Presidente Vargas Steelworks. The Miami Division threw him a rousing farewell party, with the other agents toasting him and making good-natured jokes about staying safe from the "dangerous" employees stealing office supplies and I-beams. Now he was back in Brazil as Rampart's eyes and ears in Central and South America. His father had since passed away, but the two had been able to reconnect and Roberto was glad for the time he had gotten to spend with him.

Roberto Vidal's apartment was a twelfth-floor penthouse several blocks off Avenida Atlântica and overlooking the Rodrigo de Freitas Lagoon, a five hundred-acre body of water fed by a canal that ran from the ocean. Beyond the lagoon could be seen the mountains, including the Corcovado mountain, upon the peak of which rested the iconic, 125-foot-high Christ the Redeemer statue that looked down upon the city of Rio de Janeiro.

When Kori got there, she was ushered inside by a private duty nurse, a short, chunky woman in her fifties who then led her out to the apartment's expansive deck. Roberto Vidal was seated in a chair facing the mountains with his bandaged leg elevated under a couple of throw pillows.

"Kori!" he said, turning his head around. "It is good to see you. I'm sorry I can't get up."

Roberto was tall with a toned body and a chestnut complexion. He wore shorts and a loose, tropical cotton shirt. He had deep brown eyes, a square jaw, and a few days' stubble. *If this wasn't a business call . . .* well, Kori would have to leave the thought there. At least for the moment.

"No worries, Roberto. It is good to see you, too. Let's see, the last time was in Mexico City as I recall."

"Yes. The Placido case. What fun that was, eh? Your work was stellar, as usual."

"As was yours."

"Thank you. Pull up one of those deck chairs. Oh, and there's coffee on the table. It's from a farm about two hours from here. It's strong. I think you'll like it. You'll have to serve yourself, I'm afraid."

"Of course," Kori said, pouring herself a cup of the dark roast. "I love your view."

"Thanks. Every morning I come out here and have my breakfast. And every morning I say a prayer to *Cristo Redentor* up there on that hill."

"Nice. From my place in DC, I can see the Washington Monument. Not bad, but not really anything I feel inclined to pray to." Kori grabbed a chair and slid it over next to Roberto and sat down. "How's the leg?"

"Bullet hit the meaty part of the calf. Couple inches the other way and it would have hit the bone and I'd be in real trouble. I can't put much weight on it just yet, but it will heal nicely, I believe. Hopefully, I won't get too out of shape just sitting on my butt all day."

"Oh, I'm sure you and your butt will stay in fine shape." Roberto chuckled.

"So what can you tell me about Miranda? What exactly am I heading into?"

Roberto glanced around to make sure the nurse was inside and out of earshot. "The short answer," he said, "is that you're heading into a hornet's nest."

"Hmm . . . I was afraid of that. Nothing's ever easy and straightforward, is it?"

"The country is close to revolution, Kori. Poverty and crime and drugs have finally moved the people toward revolt. A couple of factions have formed, but the leading candidate to overthrow the Estrada regime is a group that hides out in the hills outside of San Benito. They recruit in the city as well as the surrounding countryside and their numbers are growing. What was once a fledgling movement is now a formidable force. Estrada has sent troops into the hills, but the rebels know the lay of the land. It is rugged terrain and they fight with guerrilla tactics. *When* they fight, that is. For now, they run-hide when the troops come around. Then they regroup. They are waiting for their numbers to grow bigger."

"How many are in the hills now?"

"About a hundred."

"That's not very many."

"No, but they fight with passion. They fight for what they believe is a just cause. Estrada's soldiers are weak and indifferent by comparison. I would take one guerrilla soldier for every twenty government soldiers."

"Who's their leader?"

"This man." Roberto opened his tablet and showed Kori a picture of a young man with dark eyes and a full black beard. "His name is Lucas Prieto. I have met him. I went undercover as a city resident who had taken interest in the leaflets the group had printed. I went to a meeting in the basement of a church and gained the trust of one of Prieto's main men. He took me into the hills and I spent a couple of days with the group. They call themselves *El Principio*—'The Beginning.' Prieto is young, maybe twenty-four or twenty-five, but he is charismatic and smart. And I believe he is sincere. He is loved by his men. One gets the sense they would follow him anywhere."

"Is *El Principio* capable of pulling off a revolution against Alonso Estrada?"

"No. Not at this point. They are lacking any serious weaponry. But they are gaining more and more followers every day. Prieto's idea is to turn the tide of the population so strongly against Estrada that even the military will join them. Prieto believes a bloodless revolution is therefore possible."

"Interesting."

"Yes, but you see, Estrada sees it coming and is clamping down. He is a ruthless leader. The purges are back. People are being plucked from their homes. Estrada has even executed a few of his own military officers, claiming they were spying for the rebels. Whether or not they were, who can say? I don't imagine Estrada cares. He was only looking to send a message to the rest of his army."

"Lovely."

"And of course, he's started a propaganda war of his own, only he doesn't have to use leaflets. He's got control of the media. All the TV networks and newspapers are under government control. So is the internet. And Estrada is painting the rebels as everything but devil worshippers."

"I'm sure. Classic despot formula. So how did you get shot?"

"In the hills with the rebels. There was a raid by government troops. It was short and the rebels fought them off from higher ground and then escaped. I took a bullet and was carried out. One in the group was a doctor who patched me up. Then they took me to the highway, nothing more than a narrow roadway, really, that runs through the hills to San Benito to the south, and to the border to the north. They flagged down a passing truck that was going to the city and put me on it. Of course, I had to pretend that was the direction I wanted to go, but a few miles down the road, I told the driver to drop me off. Then I hitched a ride with a truck going the other direction and headed for the border. Once across, I got a ride to Porto Alegre where I checked myself into a hospital to get this thing cleaned up properly. Then I grabbed a flight back here. That was three days ago."

"And you called the chief and he called me."

"Yes. I regret that I cannot continue my investigation, but I fear I would be a liability in my current condition. If this were baseball, I suppose you'd be the relief pitcher."

"Yes, but with your good work, it looks like you're leaving the game with the lead. Maybe I can get the save, but you're still going to get the win."

"Yes, Kori, but you're taking the mound against the heart of their batting order. Things are ugly down there. Frankly, I'm not even sure what our plan should be at this point."

"Reconnaissance, for now, I guess," said Kori. "The nukes are the real concern to us. Outside of that, we can't really involve ourselves in the politics. It's not our place to take sides, as you well know."

"Of course. Rampart's directive is clear. But perhaps you will feel differently when you get into San Benito and talk to the people there. There is genuine fear of the government. It is hard not to be moved by their stories. Everyone knows someone who has been lost to the purges. There is fear, there is desperation, and saddest of all, there is widespread hopelessness. Estrada is a monster, pure and simple."

"Sure, Roberto, I understand what you're saying, but we can't go around supporting every dissident group who wants to rebel against every tyrant in the world. But I don't mind rooting for Prieto and his comrades. If you say Prieto is sincere, I believe you. Then again, as the chief points out, how do we know what Prieto has in mind down the road? Maybe he doesn't even know himself. How many times have we seen it? A revolutionary comes to power with every intention of turning his country into a free democracy. Then he gets a little taste of power and suddenly his mind changes. Hell, look at Estrada himself."

"I know. You are right, of course. What is that saying about absolute power?"

"It corrupts absolutely?"

"That's it. Yes, agreed, we must remain neutral. Our job must of necessity be limited to gathering intelligence."

"But that brings up another question. How is the CIA playing this? What are the US government's plans? Do you know?"

"There is a CIA agent down there. Oscar Rentería. I will forward you a picture of him. He is a native-born Mirandan and he has been spending time with Prieto and his group. I met him in the hills, although he had no idea who I was, of course. With my skin color and speech, I pass easily for a Mirandan. He seemed close to Prieto. If that's any indication, then I think the US government might be leaning toward the rebels. Then again, Rentería might be sidling up to Prieto only to gain intel. That would make more sense when you stop and think about it. It's no secret that the US would prefer stability to revolution. Especially since Miranda represents such an important alternative to Middle Eastern oil."

"The dollar is always going to have the last say, isn't it?"

"It would seem so. For the dollar, stability rules, even if the stability comes at the price of human rights. But, listen, Kori, there is a CIA agent stationed here in Rio named Alvin Reeves. I'm sure he's in frequent contact with Rentería. It would be worth trying to learn something of what Reeves knows. At six o'clock every evening, he stops by a Copacabana beach bar for a happy hour martini. He never misses a day. Typically, he comes alone."

"What's he look like?"

"Short, heavyset. Always wears a white Panama hat with a striped band. I'll forward you a picture of him."

"Good lead, Roberto. I'll check him out."

"He's single, too, if that helps. Thinks of himself as quite the lady's man. Maybe you could use that. I'm sure a beautiful woman like yourself should be able to get some information out of him."

"Thanks," Kori smiled. "Sounds like a great place to start."

Roberto smiled back. "I say that, of course, in the most professional of ways."

"Oh, of course. And, professionally speaking, you're not too hard to look at yourself, Agent Vidal. Professionally speaking."

"Gracias, Agent Briggs." They both chuckled lightly and then Roberto turned serious. "But speaking of appearances, Kori, have you thought about what you're going to do once you land in Miranda? I had no trouble blending in. But you, Kori? It will be more dangerous for you. How are you going to get in to talk with the rebels? Or with any government officials?"

"Great question. Supposedly, agents Darren Cooper and James Foster back at HQ are working on that even as we speak. They're concocting an entire cover story for me and I'm sure, knowing those guys, that it will be a good one. I'm to contact them later today."

"Well, however you're able to gather the intelligence needed, you must be very careful, Kori. I will give you the names of some contacts I made. Otherwise, do not trust anyone. You will be risking your life just by stepping into San Benito. Outsiders are regarded with suspicion. Nobody trusts anybody. And Estrada's men are trained to shoot first and ask questions later, if they ask questions at all."

"All part of the job, Roberto," grinned Kori.

She wasn't too worried. After all, Kori Briggs had been in dangerous places many times before and she always managed to survive. Even so, she figured it couldn't hurt to take a page out of Roberto's book. Putting down her empty coffee cup, she gazed up at *Cristo Redentor* and said a short, silent prayer.

3

Roberto invited Kori to stick around for brunch, which she was happy to do. His private nurse doubled as a cook and the two enjoyed a plate of acai berries and papaya, toast and jam, and *bolo de fubá*, a sweet cornmeal cake and Brazilian specialty.

The conversation moved away from the business at hand for a bit, with Roberto talking about his childhood in Brazil, his desire to see more of the world, and his work with the FBI. He talked about his father. Kori talked about her childhood, growing up without a father, and staying close with her mom. She liked talking to Roberto.

Then, over more strong coffee, the agents talked further about Miranda, and Roberto described his contacts, one of whom was an actual member of *Policia Nacional*. "Pablo Amador is an officer I met at a dinner party in San Benito. Over the course of a couple of weeks, we played some golf and I managed to slowly gain his trust. He told me things about the police. Bad things. He is not happy. He confessed he does not like the direction the country is going and he does not like the role the police are being asked to play with respect to Estrada's grip on power. Nevertheless, I did not come clean with him about who I was. He thinks I am an executive with Telefónica Miranda, the state-run telephone company. That was my cover. He's worth looking up. Maybe you can tell him you're my sister or something. Tell him I took ill perhaps. He's probably wondering where I've been. I believe we had even scheduled another golf game."

"Sure, I'll look him up," said Kori. "Sister, huh? Not much family resemblance."

"Hmm . . . ex-wife, perhaps?"

"That could work. But still on friendly terms."

"Of course."

"Just because you cheated on me with your secretary, doesn't mean I'd hold a grudge," Kori giggled.

"Oh?" Roberto laughed, "Well, maybe I wouldn't have cheated on you if you had paid me more attention!"

They both laughed and then decided Kori could be a sister-in-law, married to Roberto's brother Miguel.

"Yes, that sounds more plausible," Roberto concluded.

The pair chatted some more and then Kori thanked Roberto for the information and the brunch. "Now, I had better be on my way," she said.

"Of course. Will I see you before you leave for Miranda?"

"Well . . . as it happens, I seem to be free for dinner tonight, if you don't mind a little company."

"As a matter of fact, I would not in the least mind a little company. Luísa in there makes a mean picadillo."

"Sounds good. And how late does Luísa work?"

"She leaves after serving dinner."

"That sounds even better. See you at seven. I'll bring a little bottle of something."

With some time to kill before her plan to extract whatever intel she could from local CIA agent Alvin Reeves, Kori decided she might as well see some sights to make up for the ones she couldn't see in Italy. She took an Uber to Santa Teresa, an artsy bohemian neighborhood with galleries and craft stores. She wandered along the winding, cobblestone streets, taking in the old colonial architecture before finally resting her feet in a café where she ordered a caipirinha—an exceptionally refreshing drink made from distilled sugarcane juice called cachaça and considered Brazil's national beverage. It was fun playing tourist and she tried to forget for the moment that she was actually on assignment.

Afterward, she returned to the hotel, changed into a bikini with a white, crochet cover-up, and donned a wide, straw sun hat. She put on a pair of Kenneth Cole sandals and made her way down to the beach, just another vacationer strolling along the shoreline.

Ah, but is that a beach bar in sight?

The outdoor drinkery, a tiki hut with a long bar, had wicker bar stools shaded by a canopy. One of those stools held a short, heavyset man wearing a white Panama hat with a striped band. *That's got to be him*, Kori thought. *Just like Roberto said.*

Kori sat on the empty stool next to the man.

"Well, hello," he smiled, turning toward her.

"Hello," said Kori, coolly. She planned on getting Reeves talking, but she didn't want to seem too easy. She looked straight ahead, purposely not making eye contact, although out of the corner of her eye she could see Reeves's hand on his martini glass, noticing that his fingernails were dirty. *Gross*, she thought.

"Beautiful day, isn't it?" said CIA agent Alvin Reeves. "Another day in paradise, huh?"

"Yes, I suppose so."

"Are you waiting for someone?"

"No. Just looking for some shade and a cool drink."

"Well, you've come to the right place. Best little beach bar in Rio." Then Reeves motioned for the bartender. "Arnaldo? Can you set this young lady up with the drink of her choice?"

The bartender came over and said, "What can I get for you, *senhorita*?"

"Arnaldo makes the best vodka martini around," said Reeves. "If I might make a recommendation."

Kori allowed herself a gracious smile and finally glanced over at Reeves, trying not to focus on those nails. "Well, thank you, sir. Then, yes, I suppose I'll try a martini."

"Of course," said Arnaldo, going off to mix the drink.

"My name is Reeves. Al Reeves."

Kori was a little surprised that Reeves would use his own name, but then again, what reason did he have to suspect a presumably innocent tourist of espionage?

"I'm Kara Burke. Thank you for the drink, Mr. Reeves."

"Please call me Al. Or 'Big Al.' That's what my friends call me."

"Okay, Big Al. Well, thanks for the drink. Although, I must say I should be careful. I rarely drink. But, well, what the heck? After all, I *am* on vacation."

Arnoldo sat Kori's drink in front of her and she took a sip, wishing it was her customary Scotch rocks.

"Sure!" said Reeves. "Nothing wrong with knocking back a few when you're on vacation in such a beautiful place as this."

"I suppose you're right. Nothing wrong indeed. So what do you do, Big Al?"

"I'm in the finance game."

"Really? My, that sounds fascinating."

"Yes, I'm a portfolio manager for a rather wealthy clientele out of Los Angeles. Some celebrities I'm sure you've heard of, but of course, confidentiality precludes me from saying exactly who."

And there it was. If you're a CIA agent who fancies himself a lady's man, you're no doubt going to create a cover that has something to do with money or fame and Reeves had concocted a cover that included both.

"It's not as glamorous as it seems, however," Reeves sighed.

"No?"

"Well, I mean, sure the money is good. Oh, I might as well be honest; it's incredible. But, as you might guess, it's a lot of hard work and long hours. It's not by accident that you get to the top of my field working with the likes of Tom Hanks and George Clooney."

"Tom Hanks and George Clooney?" Kori widened her eyes.

"Oh, damn, I'm really not supposed to divulge names. Please forget I mentioned them. I could tell you some stories, though! Well, anyway, it's a lot of hard work. That's my point. Fortunately, I'm able to take trips like this. It's nice to get away from my place in the Hollywood Hills and come to an exotic city like Rio."

"Wow," said Kori, smiling, and leaning in toward Reeves. "You seem like you lead a *very* interesting life, Big Al!"

"Yes," Reeves chuckled. "I suppose you could say that."

"Are you here for long?"

"Um . . . just a few days. How about you, Kara?"

"Another week. Then it's back to the grind, I'm afraid. I work in the accounts payable division of a food production company outside of Indianapolis. Not quite as interesting as your line of work, is it? Anyway, I've been saving up for two years to take this trip. I've always wanted to see Rio. I was supposed to come down here with my best friend, but she got sick just a couple of days before our flight. Some gastrointestinal thing."

"Aw, that's too bad. So you're here all alone?"

"I'm afraid so."

"Well, you're not alone now," Reeves said, grinning. "How about another drink?"

"Oh, I really shouldn't."

"C'mon, another won't hurt. You *are* on vacation, you know."

"Well, I guess one more."

"Great! Arnaldo? You heard the lady."

"So, Big Al," Kori said, "as much as I love this place, with a week left in my trip I'm thinking that maybe I should visit some other locales, maybe even another country. I mean, when will I ever get to South America again, right? You seem like a very intelligent man." Reeves gave a kind of aw-shucks shrug. "What do you know about Argentina? I was thinking of seeing the Iguazú Falls. I hear they're breathtaking."

"Oh, yes, I can attest to that," said Reeves. "The falls are amazing. I have contacts there. Uh, one of my Hollywood friends. If you'd like, I can make a phone call and set you up with a nice hotel room."

"Hmm . . . maybe. And what about Miranda? I was thinking of going to San Benito. I don't know much about it myself, but I took a tour today of Santa Teresa and somebody on the tour mentioned it. They said it's a very interesting place."

"Oh, it's *interesting* all right. That would be one way to put it. Kara, I would not recommend Miranda right now. And especially San Benito."

"Really? Why not?"

"The place is in turmoil. It's very dangerous. A revolution is brewing."

"Wow, really? A revolution?"

"Yes, but it won't get far."

"Serves me right for not paying attention to the news. Well, who is it that's revolting against whom?"

"Oh, some malcontents are making things difficult for the current administration."

"How come?"

"Who knows? Something about human rights violations or something."

"I see. Wow, you know a lot about things, Big Al."

"Well, when you run a large international portfolio fund like mine, it pays to keep informed on what's going on in the world. Just part of the job, really."

"I'm sure! Well, how do you know that the revolution won't get very far?"

"Because the administration is too well-armed."

"Uh-huh. But can't the . . . what did you call them, malcontents? Can't they get weapons too?"

"Oh, sure, but they'll never have the weaponry that the people in charge of the country now have." Reeves looked around and then leaned in, lowering his voice. "Do you know how I know that?"

"How?"

"Well, let's just say I have friends in high places. The State Department in Washington."

"Really?" Kori made her eyes big again

"Yep. Secretary of state, as a matter of fact."

"Wow!"

"It's true. Anyway, I know that the rebels will never be able to outdo the weapons of the government because the United States is involved."

"We are?"

"You bet. And the US is sending weapons to Miranda's military. All kinds of stuff. Machine guns, grenade launchers, missiles, you name it."

"Wow. Why?"

"Why?"

"Yes, why is the US involved and on the side of the Mirandan government?"

"Why else? Miranda sends us close to 100,000 barrels of oil a day."

"I had no idea."

"Yep. And we don't want to risk that. Sure, maybe the Mirandan government is a little restrictive, but who knows what would happen to the oil in the hands of the rebels?"

"Sure."

"The devil you know, right?"

"Right. My goodness, Big Al. You know so much, I feel like I'm talking to someone in the White House!" *I should get an Oscar for this performance*, Kori thought.

"Can I tell you another secret?"

"Sure."

"You have to promise not to say a word to anybody."

"You can trust me, Big Al. My lips are sealed."

"Well," Reeves looked around again and his voice went even lower. "The White House doesn't even know about this."

"No?"

"Nope. It's all being orchestrated at a lower level. A certain intelligence agency, as a matter of fact."

"What, you mean like the CIA?"

"Shhh!"

"Sorry." Now it was Kori whispering. *"You mean like the CIA?"*

"I'm afraid I can't say."

"I see. Wow, this is all very fascinating."

"Well, like I said, I just try to keep informed."

"And how long has this been going on? The weapons being sent, I mean?"

"Just for a couple of weeks."

"My goodness. Big Al, you certainly are an interesting guy."

"Yeah? Interesting enough to have dinner with?" Reeves grinned.

"Sure," Kori said, smiling coyly. "Dinner with you sounds great. If you don't mind the conversation of a simple Indiana girl."

"Oh, I'm sure your life is fascinating, Kara. In its own way."

"Well, I don't know about that. Anyway, I'll need a little time to shower and change first, if that's okay."

"Of course. How about let's say we meet up an hour from now? Would that give you enough time?"

"That would be perfect, Big Al."

"There's a wonderful place on Santa Clara and Avenida Nossa. A nice, quiet place, away from all the tourists on Atlântica. I can come pick you up at your hotel first. Where are you staying?"

"Not far from there. Why don't I meet you at the restaurant?"

"Are you sure?"

"Yep. Santa Clara and Avenida Nossa."

"Right."

"I look forward to it." Kori rose from the barstool. "Thanks again for the martinis, Big Al. See you in an hour!"

"See you then, Kara."

Kori walked back toward the sidewalk and strolled in the opposite direction from the Copacabana Palace in case Reeves was watching, or worse, following. She went down three blocks, then turned at a side street and went two more blocks before turning back toward the Copa. She looked at her watch and figured she had plenty of time to shower and change before heading to Roberto's place. She'd put a call into HQ, too. And then she chuckled thinking of Reeves waiting in anticipation for Kara Burke to show up at the restaurant on the corner of Santa Clara and Avenida Nossa.

4

"Chief, I've had a productive day," Kori told Eaglethorpe when he picked up her call.

"Talk to me," Eaglethorpe said.

"Well, first of all, Vidal was a ton of help. He's given me some great contacts, including people in the rebel group as well as the name of an actual member of *Policia Nacional*, one whose loyalty to his boss is apparently beginning to wane."

"Excellent, Briggs."

"Yeah, but that wasn't the best part of the day. Get this. I managed to debrief a CIA agent stationed here in Rio, without him even knowing it."

"Nice, Kori. How did you do that? Do I even want to know? I mean, when you say de-*brief*..."

"Chief! What kind of girl do you think I am? I had an innocent drink with the man, batted my baby blues, and let him talk."

"Of course," Eaglethorpe chuckled. "So what did you learn?"

"That the CIA is working with the State Department to run weapons to Estrada."

"So the US position is to back the current regime."

"Not exactly. As it turns out, the president doesn't know."

"He doesn't?"

"Not according to CIA agent Alvin Reeves. Or 'Big Al' as he likes to be called. And I'm sure not a single Congressperson knows either."

"Then who's behind it?"

"Reeves claims a connection with the secretary of state."

"Good Lord. But why?"

"The oil. There are a lot of powerful business interests that I'm sure want to keep Estrada in power, rather than risk losing access to Mirandan oil. A hundred thousand barrels a day are imported from Miranda. Is it too far-fetched to believe that someone has gotten to the secretary?"

"No, sadly, it's not too far-fetched. But it's a pretty bold claim that we ought to keep to ourselves, Briggs. Bribery? Of a cabinet member? We don't have a shred of evidence."

"Of course, Chief."

"I should call POTUS, though."

"He'll be furious. I can see him storming into the secretary's office. And, of course, the secretary will just deny everything. Maybe we ought to play it cool. Wait until we have something more tangible to go to the president with."

"Yes, I suppose you're right. Let's keep a lid on this for now. In the meantime, maybe we can start investigating the secretary from our end."

"I think that's the right play, Chief. Besides, Vidal told me something this morning that contradicts what the CIA agent told me."

"What's that?"

"He said the main CIA spook in San Benito is a guy named Oscar Rentería, and Rentería has been getting close to the rebels, not to the regime. He's ingratiated himself with their leader, a young man named Lucas Prieto."

"Maybe he's spying for Estrada."

"Possibly."

"Well, listen, we'll dig around up here. As for you, I want you to focus on getting more intel in Miranda about both Estrada and the rebels. Let's see if we can come up with some answers and get a clearer picture of what's happening and who's in support of whom."

"Right, Chief. Speaking of which, what did you guys come up with for my cover?"

"You're a reporter with the *Washington Post*.

"Oh, yeah? I always wanted to be a reporter."

"Well congratulations, you made it. Your name is Kelly Bridges and your assignment is to write a feature piece on the political state of affairs in Miranda. We're hoping this can open some doors for you. Heck, you might even be able to interview Presidente Estrada. Of course, don't expect any honesty. If he agrees to see you at all, it'll be to use you to push his propaganda. Guys like him know how to use the press. Nevertheless, you might be able to pick up a nugget or two of information."

"Sounds like a plan."

"Cooper has overnighted you all the credentials. They'll be at the front desk of your hotel in the morning. We've got you on an 11 a.m. flight to San Benito. You'll take a taxi to Hotel San Benito, which is just a couple of miles from the presidential palace."

"Nice place?"

"I don't know, is two stars nice?"

"Two stars, Chief? Really?"

"Sorry, Agent Briggs. You're supposed to be on a journalist's expense account."

"I understand," Kori sighed. "The sacrifices I make for Rampart . . ."

"Yes, well, anyway, from there, you might try to make contact with the presidential press office. See how high up you can get. After that, you're on your own. Follow the leads Vidal gave you. At some point, you'll need to go into the hills where the rebels are. You can use the same cover. I'm sure they'll appreciate media exposure for their cause. After all, that's how Castro got the population to switch to his side in the Cuban revolution, you know. Any questions?"

"It all seems pretty straightforward."

"Great. Then get yourself a good night's sleep. Call me tomorrow when you land in San Benito."

"Roger that, Chief."

Kori didn't exactly get the good night's sleep Eaglethorpe had suggested. Dinner with Roberto had been wonderful. What came afterward was even more so. Roberto was gentle and attentive and surprisingly agile for a man with his lower leg all bandaged up. Luísa raised an eyebrow when she came in the next morning to see that Roberto's guest had stayed the night, but if she had any objections, she kept them to herself.

This time, Kori couldn't stick around for breakfast. She had to get back to her hotel, get the package Cooper had overnighted, and get herself to the airport. She had a cup of coffee with Roberto out on the deck and then rose to leave.

"Take care, Romeo," she said, kissing him on the forehead.

"You too, beautiful. And be careful down there. I'd like to see you again, you know."

"Oh, you'll see me again. Count on it."

From the hotel room, Kori called her mother to check in.

"Well, everything's just fine dear," Joan answered. "It's so nice of you to keep in touch. Wait until you hear. I had my dance class last night."

"Oh, sure. How'd it go?"

"Well, you're not going to believe it, but guess what? You know that man I mentioned? Bertram?"

"The waltzing wonder?"

Joan giggled. "Yes, the waltzing wonder. Well, the waltzing wonder asked me out on a date!"

"Really?"

"Yes!"

"That's great, Mom."

"He's taking me to Voltaggio Brothers tonight."

"Wow, nice. Sounds like a classy guy."

"Yes, he sure is. I hope you can meet him soon. Well, of course, I don't want to get too far ahead of myself."

"That's wise, Mom. See how the date goes. But have fun, okay?"

"I will."

"But not *too* much fun. Isn't that what you're always telling me?"

They both laughed and talked a little more before Kori told Joan that she was running late for a museum tour. They hung up and Kori smiled thinking of how excited her mother seemed. Joan hadn't dated anybody in years and she certainly seemed smitten by this Bertram fellow. Truthfully, at least to Kori's knowledge, Joan hadn't dated anybody seriously since her husband, Kori's father, had walked out on them. Kori was three at the time. Her father had a volatile temper and a weakness for anything in a skirt. Kori could only vaguely recall him, but she often fantasized about confronting him one day. Then again, what would she say? *Why were you such a jerk?* What would be solved by that? Still, it was always fun to think about maybe giving him a kick to the groin or at least a broken nose.

It was an uneventful three-hour flight from Rio to the Mirandan capital of San Benito, but Kori was surprised by the number of armed soldiers at Presidente Estrada Aeropuerto Internacional. The customs line moved slowly and the official reviewing Kori's passport and press credentials seemed to take forever, looking back and forth at the passport photo and Kori's face, then quizzing her on her date of birth and asking a slew of questions about why somebody from the *Washington Post* was there. Finally, he waived her through and began interrogating the next person in line.

On the taxi ride to the hotel, Kori noticed the presence of soldiers on almost every street corner. The old streets of the capital were dirty, the buildings run down and in need of paint. There were people on the sidewalks, but nobody was in any hurry to get anywhere. Bikes were plenty, but cars were few, just other taxicabs or old, rambling American cars. Homeless people rested up against vacant buildings. The contrast between Rio de Janeiro, where she'd just been, and San Benito, where she would be spending who-knew-how-much time, was startling.

The Hotel San Benito was, unfortunately, everything she expected it to be, just as rundown, just as rough. It did, however, have one thing in its favor: a bar. Not much of one, but a place where an intrepid reporter on assignment could at least get a drink. Kori checked in, dropped her bag off in her tiny room on the third floor, and then went down to the bar to order a Scotch from the bartender, an older man with white hair and beard. There were four barstools and a grand total of three tables in the place, and besides Kori and the bartender, there was nobody else around.

Kori had ulterior motives besides having a drink. In all her years of experience, she knew that nobody had a handle on any given situation quite like a local barkeep. In her estimation, the most sophisticated research and polling surveys couldn't hold a candle to a person on the front lines of the local bar and tavern scene. Bartenders always had their fingers on the pulse of the populace.

Kori took a sip of her Scotch and asked, in Spanish, "Why all the soldiers in the streets?"

"You have not been here long, I take it," the bartender said.

"Just now checked in."

The bartender looked around and then leaned in toward Kori. "*El Principio*," he said, almost in a whisper.

"Huh?"

"The rebel group. The government fears them and is cracking down. Soldiers and police are everywhere. May I ask why you are in our country, señorita?"

"I'm a reporter. From the US. I'm in San Benito to write a feature article on the political situation here."

"Things are bad," declared the bartender. "*That* is the political situation. I would be careful, señorita."

"I plan to. What's your name, señor? I'm Kelly." The bartender didn't answer. "Not for the article," Kori added. "I promise. And just a first name. So I know what to call you."

"I'm Santiago."

"Pleased to meet you, Santiago. So, tell me, off the record, where do the people stand?'

"Where do they stand?"

"Between Presidente Estrada and *El Principio*?"

Santiago glanced around again. "With *El Principio*," he said, again in a whisper.

"Why?"

"Presidente Estrada has let the people down. Look around, señorita. Look at the poverty. Not to mention the crime. The worst is that Estrada has gone to bed with the drug cartels."

"He has?"

"Everyone knows it. He is getting rich off drug money."

"I thought he made his money off oil."

"The oil money pays for the army. The drug money pays for Estrada's lifestyle. It is just one long fiesta for that man. At any given time, he has five or six mistresses. He lives in his palace and entertains dignitaries from around the world. He entertains his top generals, too, and the highest-ranking officers of *Policia Nacional*. He knows that he needs to keep them happy to stay in power. Everyone in the upper reaches of the government is an accomplice to his dictatorship. Meanwhile, the people starve. And if you dare speak out, you disappear."

"The purges?"

Santiago nodded. "The purges."

"What will happen to Miranda, Santiago?"

"Who can say? I have been around many years but have never seen things this bad. I was here when Estrada took power."

"In a coup, as I recall."

"Yes, but a peaceful one. He was the top general of the Mirandan military. The officers and soldiers all followed him. The economy had collapsed. You could not even get basic services. Power, sanitation, medicine, transportation. Estrada was a savior to the people of Miranda. He promised democracy and free elections."

"Which never materialized."

"No, but for a while, he did some good things. He built up the country's infrastructure. He built hospitals and schools."

"Devil his due, huh?"

"Then he seemed to have gone power-mad. Of course, there were never any elections. Have you seen the statue?"

"The statue?"

"Everyone talks about it. It is in the main plaza, just a few blocks from here. A fifty-foot-high bronze sculpture of our presidente."

"That seems a little over the top."

"That is Estrada. Anyway, you ask what will happen to Miranda. Only God knows such things. What will be will be. Another drink, señorita?"

"No thank you, my friend. I need to get going, I'm afraid, but I appreciate the conversation."

She paid the tab, leaving twice the amount of the drink.

"Gracias," said Santiago, picking the cash up off the bar, each Mirandan dollar with a smiling picture of Presidente Alonso Estrada.

5

— · —

Getting an appointment with the presidential press office, located in a two-story office building three blocks from the presidential palace, was easy. Unfortunately, Kori was relegated to a low-level spokesperson. She'd entered the lobby and glanced at the name board on the wall, noticing that the presidential press minister was on the second floor. That's also where the offices were for the ministers of foreign trade, agriculture, and public works, among others. Unfortunately, after telling the receptionist she was Kelly Bridges with the *Washington Post*, there for her appointment, Kori had been led into a small windowless office on the first floor. Not a good sign.

The spokesperson with whom she'd been granted an appointment, a wiry young man with a weak chin, told Kori about all the wonderful things the administration was doing for the people of Miranda, how beloved Presidente Estrada was, and how much he cared for the citizens of this great and proud Latin nation. But the words were a little too polished, talking points that had obviously been memorized and recited countless times. He may as well have just handed Kori a brochure.

She asked for some face time with Presidente Estrada himself.

"Oh, I am sorry, that would be quite impossible," the young man said. "He never talks to the outside press. Only to the Mirandan papers."

Which he owns, Kori thought. "Yes," she said, smiling, "but don't you think it would be a good idea for *El Presidente* himself to tell the world the story of his wonderful resurrection of your country?"

The young man was quiet for a moment, seemingly turning the idea over in his head. Finally, he said, "No, our instructions here are quite clear. The president does not want to be bothered by the foreign press."

"Presidente Estrada told you this himself?"

"Well, no, of course, I do not talk to Presidente Estrada myself, but I am clear on what he wants."

"I see. Well, who communicates with your office from the presidential palace?"

"Presidente Estrada's chief of staff. Colonel Tovar."

"Uh-huh. Well, maybe you can check with him. You know, the idea of getting the word out to the world about Presidente Estrada's good deeds would probably be most welcome." Then Kori leaned in and lowered her voice. "We could say the idea was yours. Be quite a feather in your cap, wouldn't it?"

Again, the young man was thoughtful for a moment and Kori was certain she'd broken through. But then he declared in a tone laden with finality, "No, señorita. That would be quite impossible. Ideas are not the province of this office. Presidente Estrada's staff knows what the president wants and they are clearly more knowledgeable as to his affairs. We in this office serve entirely at their discretion." Then, as if to punctuate his pronouncement, he stood and said, "I must wish you a good day."

Kori smiled politely and left, frustrated at being thwarted by a kid, probably no more than twenty, playing gatekeeper. He was scared, that was the problem, Kori decided. When you worked for Estrada, the best thing was undoubtedly to remain unseen. Initiative was frowned upon. You did your job every day and went home, careful not to make waves. If Kori were going to do any real reconnaissance, it would have to be good old-fashioned espionage. Just as well, she thought. That was her preference anyway. Still, she had the contacts Roberto had given her and she figured she might as well exhaust those before trying anything else.

The first was the jaded officer with the national police. Pablo Amador lived in a small, two-bedroom residence on the outskirts of San Benito with his wife. Near the hotel, Kori rented a moped and rode out to Amador's house, taking as many main roads as she could, careful not to accidentally wander into some of the rougher neighborhoods. Getting lost in San Benito was the last thing she wanted.

It was late afternoon when she arrived at Amador's house. She knocked, and a plump woman with thick, black hair framing a round face opened the door.

"*Sí?*"

"Señora Amador?"

"Sí?"

Kori smiled broadly and spoke in Spanish. "Hi, I'm Kelly Bridges." No use using her real name, she thought, even though she knew that Roberto had used his. "My brother-in-law is Roberto Vidal."

"Oh, *sí!* Roberto is a friend of my husband's. He is a very nice man. Please come in, Señorita Bridges."

Señora Amador led Kori into a modest living room. A sofa faced an old-style portable television set resting on a coffee table. Señora Amador waived Kori into an adjacent chair with a faded slipcover. At the far end of the room was a small shrine to the Virgin Mary—a covered end table against the wall with candles and a small statuette—above which hung an oil painting of the Blessed Mother. Kori guessed by the quality of it that Señora Amador might have painted it herself.

"So tell me, how is Roberto? Is he okay? He was to have played golf with my husband yesterday, but Pablo tells me he did not show up."

"Oh, yes, well, you see, that's why I'm here. I'm afraid Roberto is recuperating from an emergency appendectomy."

"Oh, my," said Señora Amador, crossing herself. "Is he okay?"

"Yes, yes, he is fine. I've just come from the hospital. He is in no condition to talk just now. However, he mentioned to me the broken golf engagement. He feels bad about it. He didn't even have time to call Pablo. Anyway, I promised him I'd swing by your place and apologize personally for my brother-in-law."

"Oh, señorita, given the circumstances, that is quite unnecessary. And we will visit him in the hospital the first chance we get."

Wow, Roberto really ingratiated himself with this family.

"Oh, no, please," she said. "You know Roberto; he would not like a fuss. Besides, he'll be home tomorrow and I'm sure he'll be in touch. In the meantime, he insisted I contact you and I was happy to come out to see you. I flew down from Miami where I live, you see, to check on him. He is married to my sister, of course."

"Oh? But I thought Roberto was single. He has told my husband so."

What was the story Roberto and Kori had agreed on? Yes, Kori was married to his brother Miguel. *Damn*, she thought, then made a quick recovery. "I'm afraid my Spanish is sometimes not so good," she chuckled. "Often I get words confused. Brother, sister, and so on. What I meant to say is that I am married to his brother."

"Oh, I see. Yes, Roberto mentioned a brother."

Nice save. "By the way, is your husband around?"

"He should be here very soon. I imagine he is on his way home from work. He is a police officer, you know."

"Yes, Roberto mentioned that to me."

"Will you stay for dinner, Señorita Bridges?"

"Please, call me Kelly."

"Of course. And you must call me Lidia. Please stay. I am making pabellón criollo. Are you familiar with Mirandan cuisine?"

"Yes, somewhat. I've learned from my husband, of course."

"Well, it is a dish of rice, plantains, black beans, and beef. It is one of Pablo's favorites."

"It sounds delicious."

"Then please stay. I have plenty."

"Well . . . if you insist."

"I do! And where is your husband now, Kelly?"

"Miguel is at the hospital with Roberto. We thought it not wise to leave him alone."

"Of course. Oh, here is Pablo."

Through the front door of the house came a portly man, built not dissimilarly to his wife. He wore glasses and sported the official uniform of the Mirandan *Nacional Policia*. He raised his bushy eyebrows upon seeing a stranger in his living room.

"Pablo," said Lidia, "this is Roberto's sister-in-law, Kelly. She is from Miami, here to visit her ill brother-in-law."

"Ill?" said Officer Pablo Amador, reaching his hand out to shake Kori's.

Lidia brought her husband up to speed on the conversation she'd been having with Kori and then informed him she'd be staying for dinner. "And so you must open a bottle of wine," she insisted. "A good one, my husband."

"Of course, of course," nodded Amador.

Over dinner in the Amador's small dining room, Pablo Amador spoke highly of Roberto; he had obviously charmed this man and gotten in his good graces. No wonder Amador felt comfortable confiding in him. Kori spoke briefly about herself, about her work as a nurse in Miami, and about her husband, Miguel. She tried her best to keep the conversation general and to deflect the more specific questions.

"Enough about me," she said at one point, "Pablo, you must tell me about your work. It must be interesting being a police officer."

Pablo shook his head. "It used to be, Señorita Kelly. Our jobs have changed, though, I am afraid. I am working no longer for the people, for their safety and security. I am working only for Presidente Estrada. We are beholden to his whims, which are, I am afraid to say, not in a good place these days. He is paranoid. He is afraid of losing power. We spend our time arresting and interrogating people who are guilty of nothing."

"Pablo!" said Lidia in a low voice. "You must not say such things out loud."

"You see, Kelly?" Amador continued, "Presidente Estrada has everybody worried. We are all on edge. As for me, I try to keep a low profile. I request street duty that keeps me away from the presidential palace and the politics of our capital. Staying uninvolved is now my preferred way of doing my job. But perhaps my wife is right. We should talk about something else. Tell me, Kelly, is Roberto's mother recovered from her hip surgery? Roberto said she was in quite a bit of pain."

"Oh, yes," replied Kori. "She's doing quite well now. She's up and around like her old self."

"I am very glad to hear it."

The conversation continued, but Kori could not bring it back around to the subject she was most interested in, namely, the inner workings of the Estrada regime.

Over coffee after dinner, Kori and Amador sat in the living room while Lidia cleaned up in the kitchen. Amador lit a cigar. "Do you mind?"

"Not at all," said Kori. "I love the smell of a good cigar."

Amador took a long puff, then leaned in toward Kori and, with a deadly serious expression, said, "May I ask you a question, Kelly?"

"Yes, of course."

"Who are you, really? And who is Roberto?"

Kori tried to hide her shock at Pablo Amador's detection of her bogus cover. Should she keep the ruse going? Act bewildered by the question? Double down and insist that she was, indeed, the sister-in-law of an executive with the national phone company? The look on Amador's face told her that her best bet was to come clean. Besides, if she had gleaned nothing else over dinner, she had gleaned that there was something about this man that spoke of kindness. Of trust. Kori decided to rely on her gut.

"How did you know?" she said at last.

"Roberto mentioned to me that his mother had passed away several years ago."

"Aha. Well, then, her hip is obviously no longer bothering her," Kori smiled. Amador did not smile back. "Look, Señor Amador, I'm sorry. Roberto and I work for a secret US intelligence agency. We're here on a surveillance mission. Roberto is not recovering from an emergency appendectomy. He is recovering at his home in Rio de Janeiro from a gunshot wound he picked up here, in a skirmish between the rebels hiding in the hills and the government forces."

"I see." Amador looked almost hurt.

"You mustn't blame Roberto. He is a good man and he had wonderful things to say about you and Lidia. But, as you can imagine, our country is very concerned about the state of affairs in your country. We are intelligence agents here to do our jobs."

"Yes," Amador said, slowly nodding. "I understand. Then would I be correct in assuming that you are on the side of the current regime?"

"Why would you assume that?"

"Because the CIA is supporting Presidente Estrada."

"So I've heard. But, you see, we are not with the CIA."

"Then who are you with?"

"I cannot say. Let's just say it's an independent organization with the ear of the president. We have not sided with anybody. We do not take sides. My job is to assess the situation and look for dangers to our country and its people. Truth be told, our major concern is Estrada's nuclear program."

"Hmm . . . I'm afraid I do not know much about that. That department is a bit above my pay grade."

"Tell me, Señor Amador, why are you still talking to me? Why are you taking such a chance? How do you know I won't turn you in to the authorities?"

"I don't," said Amador. "And I have already evinced enough doubt about Presidente Estrada's regime that, if you did turn me in, I would no doubt be summarily executed. But truthfully, it feels good to talk about these things with somebody. I am tired, Kelly. May I tell you a story?"

"Certainly. But, well, I might as well tell you that my name is actually Kori."

Amador chuckled lightly. "Of course. Well, Kori, the latest round of purges started several months ago. The rebel faction, *El Principio*, was just starting to form. Estrada was furious. He honestly believes he is a benevolent leader. But you see the way the people live in this country. You see the gangs and the violence and the drugs and the poverty. From his presidential palace, Estrada does not see these things. In fact, he has not left the palace to make a public appearance in over six months. Even if he is getting reports of the troubles in Miranda, he chooses to ignore them. When he heard about the formation of *El Principio*, it was an insult to him. He ordered the *Policia Nacional* to round up anybody who might have been even remotely associated with the rebel group. He even told us that it would be a good idea to round up a few people who weren't connected to it at all, just to put, as he said, 'the fear of God' into the citizenry.

"There is no other way to say it, Kori. We have become the Mirandan equivalent of the Nazi SS. The people we once served, the people we were once sworn to protect, now fear us. I see it in their faces. If I walk into a market or café in uniform, people are careful not to make eye contact with me. I did not become an officer of the law for this. I did not sign up to be a member of Estrada's own little SS."

Kori nodded, captivated by this man and his willingness to talk to her.

"Anyway, one night we were in Barrio Descarado, a neighborhood just on the fringes of the city. We had gotten wind of an *El Principio* meeting that had taken place in the basement of a nearby church. We were able to get the names of some of the attendees. One was a city worker. We knocked on his door and rousted him out of bed and dragged him away. There were four of us that entered the home that night, a home even smaller than this one. The wife begged us not to take her husband. I told her we just wanted to question him, but I knew better and so did she. I knew he would not survive the night. On the way out, I happened to glance into the second bedroom to see a small boy sound asleep. I remember it so well. There was a poster above the boy's bed of Marco Quezada, hero of the Mirandan National *Fútbol* Team. I do not know why seeing the boy had such an effect on me. He seemed so innocent, so pure. And I knew as we left the house that the boy would wake up in the morning without his father and that he would never see him again. A boy needs his father, Kori. That boy is destined to grow up without him. Worse, he is destined to grow up in a world where fathers can be taken from their sons at any time and for no legitimate reason other than that they attended a meeting of concerned fellow citizens."

Pablo Amador paused and collected himself before continuing. "Since then, I have requested the most menial of police tasks, walking a beat through this or that barrio. Other officers enjoy being part of Estrada's police force. They request assignments to the squads who carry out *las purgas*. They are becoming drunk with power. They see opportunity in the suffering. You ask why I am taking a chance talking to you. How can I not? If you, in any way, have the eyes and ears of your government, then you must help us. You say your group does not take sides. But you see, not taking a side against Estrada is no different than siding with him. Our country is dying, Kori. If you cannot help us, then who, in God's name, will?"

"I appreciate what you are saying, Señor Amador. And I thank you for sharing it with me. My people are afraid of the unknown. There are no guarantees that *El Principio* will bring about meaningful change, even if given the chance. Their leader, Lucas Prieto, do you know him?"

"I know of him. He is intelligent. Do you know that he attended law school? He is apparently very eloquent, too. He certainly has the attention of the populace."

"I'm sure. But we cannot be certain that he will be any better than Estrada."

"I can say with certainty that he cannot be worse."

"I understand. Well, Señor Amador, you've been very helpful. My mission is to gather information. Speaking to you has been valuable and you can rest assured that I will pass along your sentiments. But not your name, of course."

"You are welcome, Kori. And now it is getting late. It is already dark outside and I would advise that you get back to wherever you are staying before it gets too much later. This is a dangerous country after dark. I must also ask that you not come back here. Please do not misunderstand. It was a pleasure meeting you and I am glad that I was able to shed some light on our situation here. But if you are found out, if you are followed, it would be very bad for me."

"Of course."

The two stood and Amador asked, "By the way, are you armed?"

"Regrettably, no. I didn't dare try to smuggle a weapon in past airport security."

"Wait here."

Amador went into the bedroom and returned in a moment with two pistols.

"Do you have a preference?" he asked, showing them both to Kori.

"Señor Amador, this is very kind and generous of you," she said, looking over the weapons. "Well, as it happens my firearm of choice is a Glock nine-millimeter. Just like that one. If you're sure it's okay . . ."

"I insist," Amador said. "Here, let me load it for you."

"I'll make sure to return it when I leave for the States," Kori promised.

Amador handed her the Glock and she slipped it into her purse.

"Our guest is leaving, *querida*," Amador yelled toward the kitchen. Lidia came out, never the wiser about the conversation between her husband and Rampart secret agent Kori Briggs.

"Oh, must you leave so soon?" Lidia asked.

"I'm afraid so."

"Yes," said Amador, "I told her she should get back. It is not wise for her to be out too late."

"Yes, that's true," Lidia nodded. They said their goodbyes and Kori left the little home. She jumped onto her moped and headed back to her hotel with her purse across her shoulder, the weight of it now making her feel just a little less vulnerable to the dangers of the troubled nation of Miranda.

6

— . —

At a split in the main road back to the downtown area and the Hotel San Benito, Kori took a right, realizing three miles later, that she should have taken a left. She pulled over and took out her cell phone to consult the map, but unsurprisingly there was no signal. She pulled around and began heading back to the split but before long, she re-alized she must have taken another wrong turn because the street was now narrow and rough. Streetlights, casting long shadows along the road, were few and far between. *How did I get so turned around?* she wondered.

Before long she found herself riding through a small neighborhood of twenty or so dilapidated houses. Shortly, she realized the street dead-ended into a tiny cul-de-sac. From the lone street light in the cul-de-sac and a single bulb hanging down from the ceiling of the front porch of the end house, Kori could see a group of men loung-ing in chairs or leaning against the railing of the porch. She spun around and began to ride in the other direction when an ancient Cadillac Coupe DeVille rumbled into the cul-de-sac, its high beams blinding her and silhouetting her body against the dark. The Cadillac spun sideways and came to a halt, blocking her exit. She stopped her moped just before hitting the car as two large men got out of it, one of them grabbing ahold of the handlebar of the moped. Kori got off and backed away. Regaining her vision, she noticed the group of men from the porch sauntering into the cul-de-sac.

"Well, well," said one of the men from the porch, clutching an oversized bottle of liquor, "what do we have here? *Buenas noches, señorita.*"

Soon, the men surrounded Kori. She counted seven in all and she began to make a fast assessment of what she was facing. None seemed armed, giving her a distinct advantage, even though she was reluctant to use the gun. She didn't want to have to kill anyone; that was not her mission. The last thing she needed was the death of a civilian on her hands. Not that the police were likely to investigate; neighborhoods like this one were largely ignored by the police. But it was possible that the men were part of a larger gang and that was trouble that Kori didn't need. She also knew well the old truism about guns: never pull one out unless you're prepared to use it. She wondered, instead, if she could take the group using her self-defense expertise. She'd fought and subdued four men at once before, but she had to admit that seven was a little over the limit.

Her mind flashed back to her training. She thought of an instructor that everyone called "Kamikaze." The man was maniacal. "If you're faced with overwhelming numbers and you know you won't be able to beat them," he had advised, "then your best bet is to break quickly toward the least focused of the group. There's always one who's not quite ready to fight. You'll know who he is. Lunge at him first, put your index and middle finger together like this, then stab at his eye, disgorging it. Yank it out and show it to the rest of the group. I swear to God, they'll scatter like confetti in a windstorm!" And everybody knew that Kamikaze wasn't kidding. Word is that he'd done it before.

Kori hoped it wouldn't come to that. She had no interest in Kamikaze's tactic. Nevertheless, she couldn't help but wonder how she was going to dispense with this group of seven. She glanced about the men making quick calculations. The one who spoke was probably the alpha. She figured she'd have to deal with him first. The second most threatening was the driver of the car. He'd showed sinister initiative by blocking her path to begin with. Plus, the car, dinged up and run down, was nevertheless a luxury item and symbol of prestige in a neighborhood like this. That probably gave him confidence. Two of the others were standing slightly behind the rest, revealing their reluctance to get involved. They'd most likely run once Kori made a statement with the first two men. The other three were tough to read, but two of them seemed more menacing and less relaxed than the third. And the third was close by. Was he the unfocused one, the one Kamikaze talked about?

"What brings you here, señorita?" said the alpha with a grin. "You want a drink, pretty woman?"

"No thanks," Kori smiled. "Just passing through. On my way home."

"Well, don't be in such a hurry."

"Yeah," said the driver of the Coupe DeVille. "It's not polite to turn down an invitation for a drink. Don't you know that?"

"Hey, where you from, baby?" asked one of the others. "You don't look like you're from around here."

"I'm not," said Kori, again with a smile.

"You look like an *Americano*," said Alpha. "You're a long way from home, señorita."

"Yeah, guess I am," said Kori. "And as much as I'd like to stick around, I better be on my way." Maybe she could talk or charm her way out of the encirclement. She took a small step toward the moped.

"Come on, sweet thing," said Alpha. "What's the rush? We'll treat you fine. We know how to treat a lady, don't we, amigos?"

The rest snickered and Kori noticed the group slowly closing in on her. Alpha had put the bottle down and was loosening his belt. The Coupe DeVille had a long hood and Kori had a flashing thought of being thrown on top of it, helpless, her arms and legs pinned down for what seemed the inevitable assault.

Enough was enough.

To the men, it seemed as if the Glock just magically appeared in her hand, so quick and fluid was Kori's retrieval of it from her purse. She spun in a circle, pointing the gun for a split second at the face of each man.

"Who wants to be the first to get their head blown off?" she said evenly. "Doesn't much matter to me. This baby holds fifteen rounds. That means two a piece with one left over for luck."

Everyone started moving backward.

"How about you, Ace?" she said to Alpha. "Want to take one for the team? I'll bet if I send one through your ugly skull the rest of these losers would wet their pants and run home to their mommas. What do you think?"

"Hey, hey, c'mon, baby," said Alpha, trying to maintain some semblance of machismo, even with his hands involuntarily raised. "There's no reason to be like this. A pretty woman like you shouldn't even be holding a gun. You were meant for other things, baby. Come on, put the gun down and I'll show you."

Kori's eyes were on Alpha, but she sensed movement behind her. She whirled around just as the driver of the Coupe DeVille lunged for her. It was the one thing she hadn't wanted to do. She shot. But in a split-second decision, she lowered the gun and shot the driver squarely in the foot.

"Arrhhh!" he screamed, grabbing his foot and crumpling to the pavement. "You bitch! You shot me in the foot!"

"Fourteen rounds left, gentlemen," said Kori. "Where's the next one going?"

By then, several of the gang members had scattered, including Alpha. One of the others helped the Coupe DeVille driver to his feet and started dragging him away toward the porch. Soon it was just Kori and her moped. She got on, maneuvered around the Coupe DeVille, and then, to make sure nobody would follow, shot out both front tires.

A few miles and a couple of turns later, she was back at the fork where she had originally made the errant turn.

Forty-five minutes after that, she was enjoying a nightcap from Santiago at the bar of the Hotel San Benito. Sure, maybe the place only warranted two stars, but on that night, it may as well have been the Waldorf Astoria.

7

Kori needed to talk to someone in the presidential palace, preferably Presidente Alonso Estrada himself. No amount of reconnaissance would be sufficient without gaining access to the upper echelons of Estrada's government. She didn't expect to be told the truth, of course. About anything. But she knew that sometimes what you're not told is every bit as valuable as what you are told.

After breakfast the next morning, she decided on a more direct route than the presidential press office. She strode up to the main entrance of the palace itself with a legal pad in her hand and a digital camera slung over her shoulder. Armed men were everywhere. One of them stopped her at the gate.

"What is your business here, señorita?"

Kori grinned politely and showed the soldier her *Post* credentials. "Kelly Bridges," she said. "I'm expected. We're doing a Sunday feature on all the wonderful things that Presidente Estrada is doing for your beautiful nation. Can I take your picture?"

The soldier ignored the request and consulted a clipboard. "Kelly Bridges? Your name is not here, señorita."

"What? That's impossible. My secretary made arrangements with your government weeks ago. I was to be given a tour of the palace and a few minutes with the president for a photo op. We had it all scheduled for today. I've come all the way from Washington, DC. Please look closer."

"I'm sorry, señorita, but your name is not here. Have you checked in first at the presidential press office?"

"I was told there was no need. Your president's chief of staff, Colonel Tovar, told my secretary I should report here directly."

"Colonel Tovar?"

"Yes. He's the one we talked to."

"One moment, *por favor*." The guard retreated into a small guard shack and got on the phone. Shortly, he came out and said, "Please step in front of this camera, señorita."

Kori did as he said, posing in front of the security camera and surmising that the good colonel was sizing her up from his office. *Hope he likes brunettes*, she thought.

Then the guard got back on the phone. "Yes," he said. "Right away, Sir." He hung up and turned to Kori. "You will follow me, please."

The guard led Kori through the gate and into a small building with a couple of desks manned by uniformed security personnel. Then he handed one of the security officers Kori's credentials, which the officer scrutinized for a full three minutes. He made check marks on a form at his desk, then rose and ushered Kori first through a walk-through metal detector and then a body scanner. These guys were clearly leaving nothing to chance and Kori was glad she'd decided to leave the Glock back in the room. But they weren't finished quite yet.

"We need to do a personal search, as well," the officer said.

"Is that really necessary?"

"It is standard procedure. Please place your hands against this wall and spread your legs apart."

Kori did as she was told, knowing the sooner she complied, the sooner she'd be walking into the palace. The officer did his search from behind her, taking much longer than necessary and pausing a little too long over certain parts of her body.

"You know, you should think about getting yourself a girlfriend," Kori suggested.

The officer said nothing, finally handing her credentials back to the original guard and saying, "She's clear."

"Come with me, señorita," said the guard, leading her through a long corridor that eventually opened into what was, apparently, the grand foyer of the palace. And grand it was. The ceiling was at least thirty feet high with massive chandeliers hanging from it. The walls had ornate pillars trimmed in gold. The floor was marble except for a plush, red carpet that led to a dual staircase circling upward to the second floor.

"Wow, nice digs," Kori said.

Waiting for them was an army officer, evidently of pretty high rank if all the ribbons on his chest meant anything.

"Señorita Bridges?" he smiled. Finally, someone with a little personality. "I am Captain Rivera." *Captain?* thought Kori. *Cripes, how many ribbons do you get if you're a general?* "I understand you are with the *Washington Post*."

"Yes, sir."

"Very interesting. Well, we are always happy to speak to members of the American press. In fact, Presidente Estrada reads several US papers every day, including yours, the *New York Times*, and the *Wall Street Journal*."

"Well, we're flattered, I'm sure."

"I think you will find that he is a big fan of the fourth estate. It may interest you to know that he's made it his personal mission to improve our own country's media."

"Is that so?"

"Oh, yes, he's taken quite a hands-on approach. Presidente Estrada is a very proactive man."

"I see."

"Now, if you'll follow me, I will take you to see Colonel Tovar, his chief of staff."

"Will I get to see *El Presidente* himself?"

"That will be entirely up to Colonel Tovar. Please, come this way."

"Gracias, Captain."

The guard turned and departed as Captain Rivera led Kori up the winding staircase to the second floor. "All of the offices are on this floor," he explained. "The president's personal residence is on the third."

"I see."

On the second floor, he ushered Kori into a large sitting room with deep-pile carpeting and overstuffed chairs. "Please make yourself comfortable," he said. "Colonel Tovar knows you are here and I'm sure he will be with you momentarily. May I get you anything in the meantime? Coffee? Tea?"

"Oh, no thank you, Captain. I'm fine."

The captain nodded and excused himself from the room.

Kori looked around. The walls were full of enlarged photographs of the president. This was a room specifically designed to make the president's first impression for him. There he was at the ribbon-cutting ceremony of a hospital. There he was shaking hands with the president of Panama. There he was with the vice president of the United States. Greeting the pope. Addressing his troops. Making a speech in the main plaza under his fifty-foot statue. The crowning piece was an oil painting taking up most of the far wall—the president, in full military regalia astride a white horse, looking off into the distance, his expression one of acute seriousness, as though he had the welfare of the entire population of Miranda on his mind.

Behind Kori, the door opened. She turned, expecting to see Chief of Staff Colonel Tovar. But it wasn't him. The broadly smiling man at the door, not in military uniform at the moment, but instead in what was certainly an obscenely expensive blue silk suit, was none other than the man on the white horse behind her. Mirandan Presidente Alonso Estrada had entered the room.

"The Washington Post!" he boomed. "I have been expecting you." He strode into the room with a broad smile and offered his hand.

"Mr. President," Kori said, taking his hand and nodding, resisting the unconscious urge to curtsy in front of this charismatic national leader, remembering the litany of offenses she had been hearing about. Estrada was tall, broad-shouldered, and dark-haired, with a bushy mustache. "Excuse me, Mr. President, did you say you were expecting me?"

"Well, you or someone like you. I have gotten scant press from your nation's newspapers. It is quite surprising and not a little disappointing. My administration has done so much for my country. We have made gigantic strides for the people of Miranda. But where has the rightful attention been? Ah, but I knew it was just a matter of time before someone would recognize my inspirational story. Congratulations on seeing it, Ms. . . . Bridges, is it?"

"Yes, sir. Kelly Bridges." So that was it. That's how she got in. Presidente Estrada was looking for some free publicity. Maybe it was him checking her out on the security camera. He was probably champing at the bit to spread his propaganda on the world stage. Too bad the young man in the presidential press office didn't know that. She might have gotten in the day before.

"I checked with my chief of staff, Ms. Bridges, and strangely, Colonel Tovar does not remember setting up an appointment with you."

"No? Well, uh, I believe my secretary made an appointment with him through *his* secretary. Perhaps something got lost in the translation. You know how these things go."

"Yes, perhaps. But no matter. I told Tovar to have you brought in and that I would meet with you myself. Your credentials all check out and the important thing is that you are here now." Kori made a mental note to thank Cooper and Foster for the perfectly forged documents. "Permit me to escort you to my office where we can sit and talk most comfortably. I am sure you have many questions that I would be delighted to answer."

Estrada's office was an inner sanctum that one had to access by passing through an outer office where Kori noticed a desk, unoccupied at that moment, with a name plate that read: Chief of Staff Colonel Tovar. The president's office itself was an office only in the academic sense. It was nearly as grand as the grand entrance to the palace—same high ceilings, same hanging chandeliers, same ornate pillars with gold trim. But here, the marble floor was accented by islands of thick rugs. In the center of the room, on one of those islands, were posh, stuffed chairs on either side of an elaborate coffee table. At the far end of the office sat an immense desk and a chair with a ridiculously high back. Kori, who was no stranger to the White House Oval Office, determined that one could fit about five Oval Offices into the presidential office of Alonso Estrada. She noticed two presidential guards at attention along the walls, eyes fixed straight ahead, each dressed in formal military attire.

"Please, sit down, Ms. Bridges," said Estrada, waving to the stuffed chairs in the middle of the room. He took a chair across the coffee table from her and said, "Would you like something to eat?"

"Oh, no, thank you," she said. "I had a rather big breakfast."

"Are you sure? If I pick up that phone," he said, pointing to a red phone on the coffee table, "I can get you anything you'd like. Anything in the world. Just name it. Russian caviar from the Caspian Sea. Kobe beef from Japan. Lobster from the North Atlantic. The best cheeses from France. Truffles from Northern Italy. Foie gras. Oysters. The most exquisite chocolates."

"My, my," Kori said, trying to act impressed despite her awareness of the incongruous poverty of Presidente Estrada's country. "But, no, thank you, I'm afraid it would all be wasted on me."

"You will at least have a drink with me, *si*?"

Now *that* she could use. "Well, if you insist, Mr. President."

"I do!" he beamed. "What is your preference, Ms. Bridges?"

"Well, let's see, would you happen to have a good brand of Scotch around here, Mr. President?"

"Ah! A woman after my own heart. Are you familiar with Lagavulin?"

Was she ever. Not the most expensive Scotch in the world, but one of the best of the high-end brands, a sixteen-year-old rich and smoky single malt. One of her favorites.

"No," replied Kori. "I'm afraid I am not familiar with that one. Probably out of my price range. As you can imagine, we reporters have limited expense accounts."

"Well, then, you're in for a treat." He picked up the phone. "Andres, two Lagavulins."

In short order, an assistant strode in with two glasses of the Scotch on a gold-plated tray. He sat the tray down, bowed, and backed silently out of the room.

"To freedom of the press!" Estrada said, raising his glass to Kori.

"Gracias, Mr. President," Kori said, raising hers in return.

"Now, then," Estrada said, leaning back in his chair, "what I can tell you about my country? I am at your disposal and I think you'll find me very forthcoming."

"Thank you, sir. Well, to start with, my main interest is—"

"You may have heard some rumors of economic difficulties or, perhaps, of some, shall we say, limitations on certain activities, *sí*?" He leaned forward again.

"To be honest—"

"These are rumors that are spread by my enemies. They are nothing more than falsehoods, I can assure you."

"My sources—"

"In fact, let us call them what they are. Lies, Ms. Bridges. Nothing more than that."

"Some people are saying—"

"You see, I have learned that when you are on the top, you become the target of jealousy and envy. People want to knock you down. And they will stop at nothing to try to do so. They push untruths. They plant rumors. It is the nature of the position and I have learned to accept it with grace. The facts, Ms. Bridges, are that Mirandans have never enjoyed such prosperity and freedom as they do now. My approval ratings, as calculated by our most prestigious pollsters, are at unprecedented levels. My people have access to free education, Ms. Bridges. Were you aware of that?"

Well, I—"

"And I have given my people free health care, as well. But of course, you would never hear about this from my enemies. They would never mention such things. The progress my administration has made is not consistent with their agendas of fomenting trouble. Instead, they make up lies and spread them around, needlessly upsetting the people and manufacturing discord where it otherwise would not exist. It is most unfortunate."

Presidente Alonso Estrada spoke for forty minutes, pausing only to catch his breath or take a drink of his Scotch. His rambling monologue was peppered with rhetorical questions that he had no intention of allowing Kori to answer. Essentially, he interviewed himself. He spoke about his ostensible accomplishments, but was most passionate about his enemies, both seen and unseen, becoming visibly angry at times, frequently slamming his fist on the arm of his chair, his voice rising.

Eventually, it occurred to Kori that Estrada believed everything he said. Despite all appearances to the contrary, he believed his people were experiencing good times, leading Kori to the conclusion that he had either deluded himself or was being deluded by the people around him. These were, no doubt, men who feared telling him the truth, feared the repercussions of playing devil's advocates. Or who were, for their own selfish reasons, enjoying the spoils of being part of a corrupt regime and had little interest in changing the status quo or exposing it for what it was.

Further, Estrada was deluded about his enemies, making mention of the rebels, but dismissing their movement as being impotent and not at all representative of the greater population's sentiments. He was certain that the people would see through the rebels' lies. He spoke of "motivating" the people to see the truth, to see who really had their best interests at heart, and Kori realized that "motivating" was a reference to the purges. His larger concern, since the rebels were a nuisance that would soon be dispensed with, was possible betrayal from those around him. He spoke of having to "correct" some of his own staff members and Kori remembered Roberto speaking of the executions of some of Estrada's top men. "It's getting harder and harder to trust people," the president declared. "This is what happens when you have power; other people want to take it from you. But you see it doesn't work that way. Power and respect have to be earned, as I have done."

In sum, it was delusion mixed with paranoia. Trained in psychology, Kori knew that across the coffee table from her sat the leader of a country who was a danger to his people and the world. After a time, she no longer needed to see or hear anything further from Presidente Estrada, but she nevertheless allowed the discursive oration to continue before Estrada finally smiled and stood, thus signifying to Kori that the interview was over.

"Well," he said. "I have tried to answer all your questions as truthfully as possible," he smiled. "I do hope you have a much-improved impression of our country and one that you will share very soon with your fellow Americans."

"Oh, indeed, Mr. President," Kori replied. "My impression of your country is much clearer. And you can rest assured that I will be sharing my observations as soon as possible."

"Excellent, Ms. Bridges!"

8

— · —

Those observations were shared with Director Eaglethorpe the first chance Kori got. Back at her room at Hotel San Benito, she called and told him of her encounter with the president and her psychological assessment of him.

"He's crazy as a loon, Chief," she said.

"I see," said Eaglethorpe. "Is that your professional opinion, Agent Briggs?"

"Yep. Although I might also add 'nutty as a fruitcake.'"

"I'll make sure I put both in the official report."

"Seriously, Chief, this guy doesn't have a solid grasp of reality. He's convinced that his country is functioning perfectly well. He doesn't see the poverty or the crime. It's no secret that he never comes out of that palace of his. And it shows. He has *no* idea of the scope of rebellion that is brewing. He believes the rebel faction consists of no more than maybe a dozen misguided nobodies who will eventually go away for lack of interest if he doesn't have them killed first. He's genuinely fearful about those around him, however. I could sense the paranoia. He sees enemies everywhere. This is not a guy who's going to concede anything, Chief. Things are going to get ugly down here when the rebels finally make their move, especially if certain members of the military join them. Presidente Alonso Estrada will not simply step aside and go quietly into retirement. If he goes down, he's going to take a bunch of people with him."

"Why in God's name is the CIA backing this guy?" Eaglethorpe wondered aloud.

"Well, if CIA agent Al Reeves is to be believed, they're getting their direction from Secretary of State Lloyd Higgins."

"Who is, presumably, getting his direction from Big Oil."

"I think you just answered your own question, Chief."

"Yeah, I guess so."

"Speaking of the secretary, have you found anything on him?"

"Nothing definitive. Cooper and Foster are doing some digging. There does indeed seem to be a paper trail of communication between Higgins and at least two high-up oil executives. A couple of dinners and a hunting trip. But nothing illegal, necessarily. Just some evidence that he's pretty chummy with those guys."

"Where there's smoke . . ."

"I know. Hard to prove a bribe, however. I might have to have Cooper hack into his bank accounts. Look for unusual activity. Maybe something will show up there."

"Sounds like a plan, Chief."

"Now, what about the *Policia Nacional* contact?"

"I met him last night. Had dinner with him and his wife."

"Excellent, Agent Briggs. Your abilities of subterfuge are first-rate."

"Don't pin a medal on me yet, Chief. He sensed I wasn't who I said I was almost right away."

"What?!"

"It's okay, Chief. He's a good guy. A guy sick of where Estrada is taking his country."

"So what did he have to say?"

"Not a lot that we didn't already suspect. He doesn't know much about Estrada's nuclear program, unfortunately, so I'm afraid I have no new light to shed there. But he was kind enough to lend me a gun, which came in handy not long afterward."

"It did? Kori, what happened?"

"No big deal. Just a couple locals getting a little fresh."

"Yeah?"

"A minor incident."

"Be careful, Kori."

"Of course, Chief."

"So what's your next move?"

"Well, I've looked at the situation from the regime's side. I guess the next move is to hook up with the rebels. I need to go into the hills. Or, rather, intrepid *Washington Post* reporter Kelly Bridges needs to go into the hills."

"How are you going to find them in the hills? Estrada's own men can't seem to ever get a fix on them. They keep moving around. And the hills are dense, covered in forest and jungle."

"I figure I'll let them find me, Chief. I'm sure Prieto would love the publicity. Take a page out of Castro's book, as you said. Especially if he knows I've interviewed Estrada. Prieto's going to want to give his side. I just need to let word get out that the *Post* is seeking an interview with him."

"Estrada won't like that, Kori. Not one bit. And I wouldn't be surprised if he has guys tailing you to see where you go."

"I'm sure you're right. So I guess I need to find a way to let word get out, but only to the rebels."

"And how are you going to manage that?"

"I think I know a guy who can help me. There's a certain mixologist I've been handing out pretty good tips to. If he doesn't know of somebody with a direct path to Prieto, I'll bet he at least knows of somebody who knows of somebody. As good a place to start as any."

The lobby bar of the Hotel San Benito had one major flaw: it served no food. Kori was famished and resolved to eat lunch before sitting down with Santiago the bartender to see if she could somehow get herself hooked up with the rebels. Down the street from the hotel was an outdoor café that served empanadas. While she waited for her order, Kori decided to call her mother.

"Hi, Dear!" her mother answered. "Are you still in Italy?"

"Hi, Mom. Yes, for a couple more days. I'm just getting ready to sit down for a nice dinner at the hotel and thought I'd call to see how your date with the waltzing wonder went."

Joan chuckled. "It went very well. Bertram is delightful."

"That's great, Mom. Voltaggio Brothers, right?"

"Right. Oh, the meal was good. And the conversation was wonderful. Bertram is so smart. He can talk about anything. And not that it matters, Kori, but I think he's quite well-to-do."

"Really?"

"Yes. He's more or less retired now, but he was in real estate and apparently still owns a lot of property. A *lot* of property. Mostly apartment buildings around the city."

"Wow, nice. I hope you ordered something expensive!"

"Well, I did, but the funny thing is, I ended up paying for the meal."

"You offered to pay?"

"Well, not exactly. But when the check came, Bertram's credit card wouldn't work. Apparently the credit card company hadn't received his last payment because he just switched banks. You see, he thinks his accounts got hacked by an old business partner, so he's been moving his money all around. It seems like quite an undertaking. Evidently, his financial situation is very complex and, unfortunately, he's not very liquid at the moment."

"So you had to pay for dinner?"

"Oh, Kori, he's going to pay me back, of course. He's a real gentleman and seemed genuinely embarrassed. But, really, I didn't mind paying at all, I had such a good time. Afterward, we had drinks in National Harbor at a place right on the Potomac. It was just beautiful. My, it was a very nice evening. You need to meet him, Kori. I think you'd really like him."

"I'm sure I would, Mom." Kori tried to put a smile into her voice, but a little alarm sounded in her head about Bertram and his "complex" financial situation. She was probably just being overly suspicious, a constant occupational hazard.

"Are you seeing him again soon?"

"Yes, we're going out tomorrow night. He's taking me to a movie."

"Well, I hope you won't have to buy your own popcorn."

"I'm sure I won't, Kori," Joan said, with just the hint of an edge to her voice.

Kori immediately regretted the comment. "Sorry, Mom, I worry about you, that's all. I'm sure Bertram is a wonderful man. If you say so, that's good enough for me. And I'll be very much looking forward to meeting him. What movie are you going to go see?"

"There's a new Denzel Washington movie that's out."

"Well, you can't go wrong with Denzel."

"Right?"

The two talked some more and then when the empanadas hit the table, Kori said her dinner had arrived.

"Gotta go. It was great hearing your voice. Love you, Mom."

"Love you, too, Dear."

"Give Bertram my best!"

Half an hour later, back at the hotel bar, Kori was relieved to see that, once again, nobody was around but Santiago.

"Scotch, señorita?" Santiago offered as Kori took a seat at the bar.

"Maybe something a little more refreshing and thirst-quenching, Santiago. You got a good local beer?"

"*Sí*. Try this. It is a pale lager made about three miles from here." Santiago poured two fingers of a draft beer into a glass and sat it in front of Kori who sipped it and nodded her approval.

As he poured a full glass for her, she said, "So, Santiago, did I tell you why I am here?"

"You mentioned you are a reporter, señorita."

"That's right. *Washington Post*." With that, she laid down her fake US press agency ID. Santiago glanced at it. "I'm thinking you might be able to help me, Santiago."

"Me? How so?"

"I need to interview someone with *El Principio*. Maybe even Lucas Prieto himself. I'm afraid my boss is insistent.

Our goal is to get a real feel for the mood of the people and the leader or leaders of any dissenting political factions."

"I see. And how can I possibly help with such an endeavor?"

"I have a feeling you know some people, Santiago. Some people who might be able to lead me to Prieto. And I think he would want to meet with me. I can offer him something he can't get with his weapons and soldiers. I can offer him and the rebel cause free exposure. I have seen enough of Miranda to suggest that an article on the forces opposing Presidente Estrada would be a favorable one. At the least, it certainly wouldn't hurt for him to talk to me."

"What makes you think I know anyone involved with *El Principio*, señorita? I am but a poor barman merely trying to make it through each day. I keep my nose clean and I stay out of politics. The problems of the country are not in my department."

"Aren't they? I heard you speak the other night, Santiago. You spoke to me with disgust of Estrada and his lifestyle. You talked about the poverty here. You are not happy with the direction of your country, Santiago."

"Perhaps not."

"And I have a hunch that you know a lot of different people. This bar is empty this afternoon, but I know that at night, it's often a go-to place for many people here in the downtown. Important people?" Kori leaned in. "You can trust me, Santiago. More than you know. I just need a contact. Someone who might know where the rebels are. A name. I'll do the rest."

Santiago was quiet for a time and Kori let him be so. He was mulling things over in his mind and she didn't want to oversell.

Finally, he glanced around the bar and then, almost in a whisper, he said, "I cannot give you a name, señorita. However, I can pass along yours to the right person. Come back later tonight. I will have some news for you then."

"Fair enough, Santiago. Gracias."

"I cannot promise anything, señorita."

"I understand." Kori rose and dug into her purse for some money to pay for the beer.

"No, señorita. The beer is on the house."

"*Gracias, mi amigo*," Kori smiled. "I will see you later."

9

—·—

Kori whiled away the afternoon strolling around downtown, but never straying far from the hotel. San Benito was not the kind of city one meandered aimlessly around, popping into shops and art galleries or sitting in cafés having fancy drinks. Even in the light of day, there seemed to be an air of danger. And then there were the armed soldiers on the street corners, an ever-present reminder that the country was basically in a state of siege from its own government. One feared the soldiers more than one feared the ubiquitous threat of crime.

But Kori strolled with a purpose, testing Eaglethorpe's belief that she'd be followed by members of Estrada's police force. And indeed she was. One presumably plainclothes police officer remained thirty yards behind her at all times, making every turn she made. She pretended she didn't see him and instead let him follow her. An innocent journalist would have no reason to believe she was being followed. Finally, she returned to her room at the hotel, glancing out of her window to see the man leaning behind a lamppost in the street outside.

Kori watched a little TV, four channels, all government-run, one a news station with a smiling woman delivering happy reports about the wonderful things going on in Miranda, and the remaining three showing bland soap operas or game shows. She turned off the TV, read a little of a Joseph Campbell book she'd brought with her, then took a nap. Eventually, as evening came and the sun began to set, she ordered dinner from room service, a rice and beef dish with black beans that was blander than the soap operas. Peering from behind the window blinds, she could see the man was still outside, although by now he had given up leaning against the lamppost and was instead sitting on a bench, comfortable in the apparent belief that Kori had no idea he was out there.

Finally, Kori made her way back down to the bar, leaving the light on in her room to make the man outside believe she was still there. The bar held a few more people on this night, but it was still Santiago serving the drinks.

"Scotch, señor," Kori said, taking a seat at the bar and sensing that Santiago would prefer that she not let on that she knew him. "Straight."

"Of course, señorita," he replied, pouring her a glass. "Would you like to charge it to your room?"

"No, I think—"

"Of course, I'll be happy to charge it to your room."

"Sure," said Kori, following Santiago's lead, although she had no idea where he was going with it. "That would be fine."

"And your room number?"

"302."

"302," he repeated. "Very good, señorita."

Kori took a sip of her Scotch and looked around. Behind her at one of the tables was a young, brightly dressed couple sharing a bottle of wine, probably guests at the hotel on vacation, making Kori wonder who would choose San Benito, Miranda, for a vacation spot. *Well, you don't have to put up with throngs of other tourists,* Kori thought, *and when you're young and in love, does it really matter where you go?* At another table sat a middle-aged man in a suit whom Kori presumed was a traveling businessman. *Even in turmoil, there are business opportunities,* she imagined. *Maybe especially in turmoil.*

At the other end of the bar sat a man with a goatee and black-rimmed glasses finishing a beer. Santiago turned his back to the bar and Kori noticed him writing something down. Then he nonchalantly turned around and sat a napkin next to Kori's drink, an ordinary cocktail napkin. Kori let it sit for a moment and then casually turned it over to see a message written on the back.

The man at the end of the bar will come to your room. Wait ten minutes.

Santiago turned toward the man as the man took the last swallow from his beer glass and asked, "Another, señor?"

"No, gracias," said the man, reaching into his pocket for some bills which he placed onto the bar. *"Buenas noches."*

"Buenas noches," Santiago nodded.

The man left the bar and Kori checked her watch. Then she ordered one more Scotch. Ten minutes later, she paid her tab. *"Buenas noches,* señor," she said to Santiago. She walked out of the bar and took the stairs up to her room.

She wondered at the level of care exhibited by Santiago and the man at the end of the bar to make sure nothing more than casual bar conversation between them could be observed. Were they suspicious of the businessman? The couple? Were they worried about secret, government-installed cameras? Fear, it seemed to Kori, was the predominant currency of San Benito.

She waited inside her room and very shortly there was a light knock on the door. She opened it and the man with the goatee and black-rimmed glasses slipped inside.

"Kelly Bridges?" he said.

"Yes."

"*The Washington Post*?"

"Yes." She dug her press ID out of her purse.

"You wish to see Lucas Prieto."

"Yes. For an interview."

"Comandante Prieto knows who you are. He would welcome you. My name is Domingo. Come with me. There is a vehicle waiting downstairs."

"I think you should know that I'm being followed," said Kori. "At least I think so. Look out the window. The man on the bench. Do you see him?"

Surprisingly, Domingo opened the blinds, seemingly oblivious to the risk of being spotted. But then he waved down to the man, who waved back. "He is one of ours," Domingo said. "Our apologies. We needed to surveil you. We can take no chances."

"Of course. I understand."

"That is not to say that Estrada might not be having you followed as well, but we have seen nobody all day long. Have you interviewed him for your paper?"

"Yes, this morning."

"We assumed as much. Estrada is a believer in his own lies. He probably believes he has charmed you and made you believe he is the second coming of our Lord. He cannot conceive that you would write anything negative about his regime. You are not a perceived threat to him."

"I imagine you're right."

"Come on. We have a long trip ahead of us, señorita."

Behind the hotel, Domingo and Enrique, the man who had been tailing Kori all day, helped her up into the back of an old Dodge box truck, circa 1970. Domingo had frisked her in her room and searched her purse but had found nothing on her. Kori knew better than to try to bring the Glock along. What would a journalist be doing with a loaded weapon?

"There is room in the cab only for me and Enrique," explained Domingo. "Besides, no offense, señorita, but we have orders not to allow you to see where we are going. For security reasons."

"I understand."

"There is a mattress you can sit on. The ride is about three hours up into the hills. We take back roads and the roads are not very good, I'm afraid. I trust you will not be too uncomfortable."

"Don't worry about me, Domingo. Let's get this puppy moving."

The men closed the rear doors of the truck and Kori found herself in total darkness. She pulled out her phone and used the light to sweep around the eight foot by eight foot cargo box, seeing the mattress in the corner, along with boxes of canned goods, bottled water, and other food supplies. There were cartons of medical supplies, too, and Kori surmised that the truck was probably shuttled routinely between San Benito and the rebels' camp, smuggling provisions to the men. *Dangerous work,* Kori thought. *Surely, Estrada's soldiers and police officers make it a habit to randomly search trucks leaving the capital. That explains why Domingo and Enrique use only back roads.*

The truck suddenly lurched forward and Kori fell back, slamming into the rear door with her shoulder, grateful that the door didn't give way and spill her into the street. *Guess I'll sit down.* She made her way to the mattress, rubbing her bruised shoulder.

As the truck rolled along, Kori tried to find their location on her phone but was unable to get a signal. No wonder the men let her keep the phone. It was useful now only as a flashlight. Instead of following their route on an app, she took notes of the turns the truck made and, using her watch and estimating their speed, tried to calculate the distance between them. But the attempt soon proved futile. By the sway of the truck, she could tell a hard left turn from a hard right turn, but anything in between was difficult to discern. At times, it seemed as if the truck was going in circles. Eventually, she gave the exercise up.

For two-and-a-half hours, Kori sat on the mattress, the truck bouncing up and down over roads that only got worse the farther from San Benito they went. Ruts and potholes were such that Kori wondered if they were driving on actual roads at all. The truck continued winding around, going up and down hills, eventually taking hills so steep she could hear the truck's engine strain and felt herself being pulled toward the rear of the box.

On a level piece of ground, she felt the truck slow and come to a halt. Were they at the camp? Kori heard voices outside, gruff and loud, but from inside the truck, she could not make out what was being said.

Then a voice got louder still.

"Salir del camión!" Someone was apparently commanding Domingo and Enrique to exit the truck. The order was angry and forceful. Whoever stopped the truck was clearly not of Prieto's band of rebels.

The next sound Kori heard had her diving underneath the mattress. Rapid-fire gunshots broke out and went on for several seconds. She could hear broken glass and bullets penetrating the metal cab in front of her.

Then the firing stopped and all was quiet.

A few moments later, she heard voices coming around toward the back of the truck.

"Abre la puerta," said one of the voices, a voice that didn't belong to either Domingo or Enrique. "Open the door."

The handle turned and from underneath the mattress, Kori could hear the squeak of the metal doors being pulled open. She flattened her body under the mattress as much as possible and held her breath, never in her life feeling the absence of a gun more than at that moment.

10

A conversation in Spanish took place between two men.

"Supplies," one of the men said. "You were right. They were rebels. We should have followed them instead of stopped them. They were probably going to their camp."

"Yes, but how were we to know? We have orders to stop and search trucks like this."

"Not this far out. We're in the middle of nowhere. It was an accident that we were even here."

"Nevertheless, it is good that we stopped them. One less truck of provisions and two less rebels." They both chuckled. "Besides, this is as close to the rebel camp as I care to be. I did not sign up for a war when I reenlisted. Let others fight for Estrada."

"Agreed. So what are we supposed to do with this stuff?"

"Leave it. We'll call it in. But we should disable the engine first. Come on."

Kori heard the footsteps of the men go around to the front of the truck. A few minutes later, she heard two car doors slam and then the sound of a vehicle driving away. She waited a full minute and then slid out from under the mattress. She walked to the back of the truck and peered outside. It was still dark, but by the light of the moon, she could see that nobody was around. She hopped down from the truck and made her way to the cab to see the bodies of Domingo and Enrique sitting where they had been shot. She took a deep breath to collect herself, then looked through the cab for their guns but came up empty. Surely, the soldiers had taken them. Had Domingo and Enrique even had time to reach for them? Or were they shot in cold blood?

Under the hood, Kori noticed that the distributor cap had been removed. She knew she had to move on. But to where? She figured they had been two-and-half hours into their three-hour trip, so they were still a half hour by vehicle from the camp. They probably hadn't been averaging more than thirty miles an hour over the rural roads; that meant they were still fifteen miles or so from their destination. She could continue by walking along the road, but it was too much to hope that the camp was a straight shot ahead. Still, what choice did she have?

Kori grabbed a couple of bottled waters from the back of the truck and started walking. The road underfoot was mostly gravel. Thick trees and deep vegetation along the sides of the road made it so dark that Kori could barely see more than ten feet into the tropical forest that covered this part of the hills. The silhouettes of the trees against the moon seemed ominous and vaguely threatening.

The network of roads in these hills was designed for the express purpose of getting one through the area, not to lead one to it. Nobody would have any reason to be where Kori was walking unless they were passing through to someplace else. And at this time of night, nobody would have any reason to be passing through. There were no vehicles, no street lights, and as far as Kori could tell, not a single person within miles of her. By habit, she took out her phone to check her location and put it away when she saw, predictably, that there was no service.

The moonlight allowed her to at least see the road in front of her and she continued, listening to all manner of jungle sounds coming from the trees. She knew there were spider monkeys in Miranda and too many tropical birds to name. She also knew there were venomous coral snakes and the occasional jaguar, neither of which she had any interest in seeing up close and personal.

After an hour, the road started making a steep incline and Kori found herself breathing hard and feeling the burn in her thighs. A few hundred yards later, the road began to level off again, but Kori knew she was now at a fairly steep elevation. Despite the darkness, she frequently looked closely to the sides, making sure not to miss a turnoff that might lead to the rebel encampment. But the road continued.

After two hours of walking, the road narrowed and she came to a fork. She took the left route for a hundred yards or so but could only guess at the road's eventual outcome. She doubled back and walked the right path with the same result. She went back to the fork and considered both paths. Which led to the camp? Which would go on for miles and miles and possibly lead nowhere? She sat down to rest, taking a swig out of the second water bottle, having already consumed the first, and caught her breath.

Finally, she stood, knowing she had to make a choice. She thought about her training—the survival skills, the orienteering and navigational coursework—and decided that none of it would help her predicament.

"There's only one thing to do," she said to herself. "The only logical, intelligent, practical way to proceed." Then she began pointing her finger alternately left and right as she recited, "One potato, two potato, three potato, four; five potato, six potato, seven potato, *more*. Aha! Right it is."

Two miles down the right-hand route, the road forked again. This time, the turnoff was a much narrower road and the gravel became dirt. Kori took out her phone and got down on her hands and knees. Using the flashlight app, she scrutinized the surface of the dirt road turnoff. There were tire tracks, even footprints. She had no idea how old they were, but she knew that conditions in the jungle changed rapidly. That the tracks and prints were still visible was a positive sign that whatever traveled down this road, it must not have been very long ago.

She began walking down the dirt trail, a trail wide enough for a single vehicle. The sky was lightening a bit. Dawn was breaking over the hills of Miranda. Kori could better make out the trees and landscape. The trees seemed less threatening now, even as the trail began to extend into thicker and thicker vegetation. For thirty more minutes she walked, following the trail and the tracks of whatever had recently utilized it. She thought of her whirlpool tub in her DC apartment and imagined how good it would feel to be soaking in it. Or at least soaking her sore feet.

Finally, with the sun rising through the trees, she sat down and finished her remaining water. She looked at her watch, promising herself she'd rest for no longer than ten minutes, no matter that she felt beat and physically spent. And that's when she heard the unmistakable sound of the bolt action of a Barrett M95 rifle.

"Señorita," came a voice from behind her. "Do not move."

Kori raised her hands and a young bearded man with an intense expression and dressed in a soldier uniform came around to face her, pointing the Barrett at her head.

"*Buenos días*," Kori smiled. "Lovely morning for a walk, don't you think?"

"Who are you, señorita? What are you doing here?"

Kori took a close look at the uniform. It was ragged. There were no patches signifying rank. No insignias, no ribbons, no markings of any kind. This was not a government soldier. This young man was a rebel guerrilla. A soldier with *El Principio.*

You can't beat one potato, two potato, thought Kori.

"My name is Kelly Bridges. I'm a reporter from America, here to do a story on your movement. I am to interview Comandante Lucas Prieto."

The soldier lowered his weapon. "My name is Carrera. Comandante Prieto was expecting you last night. Where are Domingo and Enrique?"

"I'm sorry, but we were stopped by government soldiers. Your comrades were shot, I'm afraid. I hid under a mattress in the back of their truck and escaped on foot."

"Domingo and Enrique were . . . killed?"

"Yes. I'm sorry."

"Those government bastards," the young man seethed.

"From what I could hear, they tried to make a decent fight out of it, if that's of any consolation."

"Of course they would. Where were they shot?"

"I wish I could say. I've been walking for around three hours from where it happened, if that helps."

"Okay. Follow me, señorita."

Kori and the young rebel guerrilla walked for another half hour, taking several turns that made Kori grateful that she had been found. After all, statistically speaking, *one potato, two potato* is bound to eventually fail. In time, the two came to a clearing about half the size of a football field. Stretching out in front of them was a collection of tents and several well-worn vehicles, including a jeep, another box truck, and a couple of pickup trucks. The tents surrounded a large campfire that someone was cooking over. Kori smelled bacon and suddenly realized how famished she was. On the outskirts of the camp, two guerrillas posted as sentries questioned Carrera about Kori's presence, and then one of them jogged off toward one of the tents. A few minutes later, he returned.

"Come with me, señorita," he said. They walked into the camp and the sentry led Kori to a different tent, this one empty, but for a cot. "Comandante Prieto has asked that you wait here. He will see you later today. In the meantime, you must be hungry. And thirsty. I will bring you breakfast. You can rest afterward. Carerra tells me you have been walking through the night."

"I have. Something to eat and drink would be most welcome. Gracias."

The man left and returned a few minutes later with a large thermos of water and a plate of bacon and scrambled eggs. Kori ate her fill, then kicked her boots off and lay down on the cot. *Best room service ever*, she thought hazily before drifting off to a sound sleep.

11

— . —

"I hope, Señorita Bridges, that you can see what we are dealing with."

El Principio Comandante Lucas Prieto was holding court from a folding chair outside his tent, several of his men gathered around him. Kori, as Kelly Bridges, *Washington Post* reporter on assignment, was seated across from him on a log, diligently jotting notes into a notepad. She had slept well for several hours. After waking, she'd grabbed her notepad and requested that her promised interview with the rebel leader commence. Prieto was happy to oblige.

"Domingo and Enrique were good men," Prieto was saying. "They had families. And Estrada's men killed them in cold blood. They must not have died in vain. You must tell the world what is happening down here. Domingo and Enrique are just the latest. Do you know of the purges?"

"Of course."

"Hundreds of people have been killed in cold blood by Estrada and his bloodthirsty henchmen."

Kori glanced around the circle and noticed that the men sat in rapt attention. It was no wonder. Though young, Prieto spoke with the quiet authority of a seasoned leader. Physically, he was a big man, bordering on overweight, but he carried his weight well on his large frame. His full black beard made him appear even larger. He wore a simple khaki uniform and cap, just like Carerra, just like all of them. The guerrilla band made use of rank, but no soldier's rank, even Prieto's, could be discerned by their attire. Around Prieto's waist was a gun belt. A worn leather holster housed an old Remington M1911 pistol.

"No doubt you have seen the violence and the crime, Ms. Bridges," Prieto continued. "The government is inept, incapable of taking care of its citizens. This would be bad enough, but it is not just the incompetence that is dangerous. It is the venality and corruption of most all of Estrada's administrative officials. I doubt that there is an honest person in his government. Estrada's money comes from your country's oil companies and from my country's drug lords. Estrada is a drug lord himself, in truth. But he covers it. All his dealings are done through others. He tries to present himself as an honest, God-fearing man. But make no mistake. The drug money flows to him."

"What can you tell me about his nuclear program?" Kori asked.

"He has nuclear weapons. And he has some of the top scientists from Miranda working on missile capabilities. My sources tell me they are very close to being able to launch a warhead. Once his program gets to that point, it might be too late to stop him. And there are still other weapons of mass destruction to worry about, Señorita Bridges. Are you familiar with sarin gas?"

Of course, she was. Kori knew all about the colorless, odorless liquid nerve agent. After direct inhalation, it can cause death within two minutes. Saddam Hussein had used it in Iraq against the Kurdish city of Halabja. Over five thousand had been killed. It had been used in Aleppo in the Syrian civil war, killing dozens. A Japanese terrorist group had released it in a Tokyo subway, killing twelve and injuring thousands.

"Not really," she said.

"It is a deadly nerve agent that Estrada's scientists have been developing. We fear that Estrada would not hesitate to deploy it against us, or even against those citizens of our country who are politically neutral. He could even use it on entire districts or barrios if he believes there are enough dissidents within. What does he care if innocents are killed, too? Even children?"

"And where is he developing these weapons?"

"The Ministry of Science operates out of a large industrial building south of San Benito. It is heavily guarded. I will give you the address so that you can see for yourself. But we have spies within. We know what is going on in there. You see, *El Principio* has eyes everywhere. What you observe with this camp, Señorita Bridges, is the tip of the spear. We are all of Miranda. We are in the hearts of the people. There are groups of us throughout the country, meeting in secret, recruiting more and more people to our side. You should think of this camp as the military branch of a very large movement. For every one of us with a gun, there are a thousand with the will to join the coming revolution. We are everywhere. That is how I know we will be successful. Yes, it might take time, but we will prevail in the end."

"And what are you promising the people, Comandante Prieto? As an alternative to Presidente Alonso Estrada, what are you able to offer Mirandans?"

"A democracy instead of a dictatorship. Safety instead of fear. Peace instead of violence. Life instead of death."

Prieto was certainly eloquent. Roberto had called him "sincere," and she found herself in agreement with the assessment.

Prieto spoke for another full hour, openly answering Kori's questions. He spoke of his background, growing up poor but managing to secure a scholarship to play baseball at the University of San Benito where he studied law. But then Estrada's grip tightened on all facets of the country and he closed the universities to all but a select few, like those who went to work in the Ministry of Science. For the great majority of the population, Estrada decreed that higher education was a waste of time and money. People were needed in the fields and factories. The ordinary worker was exalted. The intelligentsia and financial elites were considered a drag on the country. Prieto's dreams were broken and he believed that Miranda was heading in the exact wrong direction. From that point on, he became driven to do what he could to unseat Estrada from power. There were others and they soon formed *El Principio*. Prieto was unanimously elected leader. They published anonymously online until Estrada essentially shut down the internet. Then they started printing the leaflets and holding secret meetings. Eventually, many of them armed up and took to the hills, now a full-fledged revolutionary force. They stayed on the move. The current campsite was settled only the day before and Prieto planned on moving elsewhere probably in another day.

Kori listened intently. "But what is the long-term plan?" she asked. "How do you go from where you are now to where you can overthrow Estrada?"

"I will not lie to you, Señorita Bridges. We need help. We beseech the United States. Your country is a bastion of freedom. A lighthouse pointing toward individual liberty. We have made overtures to your people. Through your country's embassy, we have formally reached out to your state department. But they have ignored us."

Of course they have, thought Kori, thinking of the secretary of state.

"We are hoping your feature story on our cause will help," Prieto continued. "Once the great people of your nation read of our plight through your eloquent words, perhaps they will mobilize your government to action."

"Yes, perhaps," said Kori. She felt a twinge of guilt that this group's leader was putting so much stock in her ruse. Nobody was going to read about Miranda's plight. Then again, Kori also knew that Rampart, if so moved, could do more for the country of Miranda than any newspaper ever could. If Prieto knew the truth, he'd be happier with the idea of Kori as a Rampart agent than as a newspaper reporter.

"You see, we need arms," he added. "We need a show of force such that the fear of God gets put into Estrada's people. But we hope not to have to use such a force. We remain confident that once Estrada's generals see the direction of the people, their resolve to form a new government, they will abandon Estrada. Especially if we are recognized by the United States as a legitimate government in waiting. Without the army behind him, Estrada is nothing. We pray for a peaceful transition to a new, democratic regime."

"But failing that," came a voice from behind Kori, "we are prepared to go to war and take the government by force!"

Kori spun around to see a tall, muscular man with short, jet-black hair and a thin mustache grinning at the group.

"Fernando!" exclaimed Prieto with a broad smile. He rose and strode over to the man and embraced him.

"Señorita Bridges, may I introduce you to my second-in-command? My right-hand man and compadre, Fernando Vallejo!"

Kori stood and shook the man's hand, sensing that she'd seen him before somewhere. *But where?*

"Señorita Bridges," Vallejo said, nodding. "To what do we owe the pleasure?"

"Señorita Bridges is with the *Washington Post*, Fernando," Prieto explained. "She is doing a story on us. It may well give us the legitimacy that we need."

"Is that so?" said Vallejo. "A reporter from the *Washington Post*, eh?" Was it Kori's imagination, or was there just a trace of skepticism in Vallejo's tone?

"You have come from the city, Fernando?" said Prieto. Then turning toward Kori, he said, "Among other things, Fernando does reconnaissance for us. One must know what one's adversaries are up to at all times. I trust your trip went well, my friend. What news do you have?"

Vallejo glanced at Kori and said, "Perhaps we should discuss it privately, Lucas."

"But of course. In the meantime, please, sit. I'm sure Señorita Bridges has some questions for you."

"Fire away, Señorita Bridges," said Vallejo, taking a seat next to Prieto. "But for reasons that will become clear, I must insist that everything I tell you be off the record."

"Off the record?"

"Or I will have nothing to say."

What the heck, thought Kori. *It's all off the record, anyway*. "Sure, I understand." She made a show of closing her notepad and putting her pen away. "Well," said Kori, "how did you two meet?"

"Fernando came to me six months ago," Prieto said, answering for his second-in-command. "He was with the government."

"Ministry of internal affairs," Vallejo added. "Deputy assistant to one of the Minister's top advisors. A good position at one time. But I have seen the degradation of the government, the deterioration of any pretense of integrity. I could not, in good conscience, remain involved. And so I joined *El Principio*. I left the ministry saying that I wanted to spend more time with my family. But I have kept my relationships there."

"At great personal risk," Prieto interjected.

"Those relationships are advantageous to our cause. I continue to know the secrets. Where the bodies are buried. What the plans are. Where the dangers lie."

"And nobody suspects you are part of *El Principio*?" Kori asked.

"Nobody. Which is why this conversation is off the record."

"My friend has become extraordinarily valuable to us," said Prieto, "as I'm sure you can imagine."

"Of course."

"Why do we share this with you?" said Prieto, now taking control of the interview again. "It is because I want you to understand that we have talented people and valuable resources. We have excellent intelligence on Estrada and his corrupt regime. We are not an amateur group of feckless dissidents. We are a strong and capable army, perhaps not in military numbers yet, but we are getting stronger every day. We are a group who can win. And a group who can lead. With your country's help, of course."

"I see."

"Now, my friend here would tell you that we are already strong enough to strike in military fashion. He wants to take the battle to the capital, don't you, Fernando?"

"It is the only way," said Vallejo. "Comandante Prieto here believes in a peaceful solution. He assumes the government will fold in the face of public dissension, that Estrada will simply hand over the keys to the palace. History shows that peaceful solutions never work. Look at your own country's revolution, Señorita Bridges."

"We shall see," smiled Prieto, slapping Vallejo on the back. "It is the only thing we disagree about. Yes, it is a big thing, but Fernando here is a loyal friend and soldier. We will see what the future brings. Perhaps we will win by peaceful means. Perhaps we will be forced to fight. Now, Señorita Bridges, I must ask that we close this interview. It has been a pleasure for me and I thank you for your interest in our nation's affairs. You are welcome to eat with us this evening and stay the night. I will have one of my men drive you back to the city first thing in the morning."

"Gracias, Comandante," said Kori. "I have very much appreciated your time with me. It has been enlightening."

Back in her tent, Kori made mental notes of her impressions, knowing that impressions can become skewed with time. She needed to understand her own instincts, what they were telling her, what they meant.

Her overwhelming sense was that Prieto was the genuine article. He spoke with passion and fire. The aspect of the interview that concerned her, however, was the addition of Fernando Vallejo. Prieto called him his second-in-command, but she noticed that Vallejo called Prieto by his first name. They seemed more like buddies than comandante and subordinate. And the story of working in the ministry of internal affairs seemed off. Vallejo quit, citing his desire for more family time? But maintained his relationships and took frequent trips between the capital and the hills? As if Estrada's police force wouldn't surveil a former member of the government. And "off the record" or not, why would he take the chance of exposing his true identity to a member of the American press? Just to show that

El Principio has access to valuable intelligence, as Prieto claimed?

No, something didn't add up. And where had Kori seen him before, anyway? Then it occurred to her. She took her phone out and scrolled through the information and pictures that Roberto had forwarded to her back in Rio. And there it was, a picture of Fernando Vallejo. The jet-black hair, the pencil-thin mustache. Only Fernando Vallejo wasn't his real name. And he hadn't been a deputy assistant with the Mirandan Ministry of Internal Affairs, either. His real name was Oscar Rentería, and he was an agent with the United States Central Intelligence Agency.

12

Dinner at the camp that night was simple. Black beans and rice. The men spread out around the camp, but Kori was invited to eat privately with Prieto and Rentería, a.k.a. Vallejo. Prieto produced a bottle of rum which the three washed their meal down with. Kori worried the conversation might turn personal, in which case she'd have to ad lib the background and personal life of Kelly Bridges, but Prieto dominated the discussion, talking about the future of Miranda and his vision for a free and democratic country. He covered much of the same ground as he had earlier in the day, but he never seemed to say the same things in the exact same way. These were not talking points he was rattling off. These were deeply held convictions.

Meanwhile, Rentería let Prieto talk. Maybe it was Kori's imagination, but Rentería seemed much more reticent than he had earlier, as if he were being careful about what he might say. And the rum didn't seem to loosen him up.

Eventually, she bade the men goodnight and retreated to her tent. She set her phone alarm for 2 a.m., put it on vibrate, and placed the phone on the ground next to her head. She managed to get a few hours of deep sleep before the alarm went off. She shook herself awake, needing several seconds to get her bearings and remember where in the world she was. The inside of her tent came into focus and she remembered why she'd set the alarm: it was time to do a little after-hours investigatory work.

During the day, she had made careful note of the design of the camp. There was one tent in particular that stood out to her, a larger, dome-shaped tent that had remained closed the whole day. She never saw anyone entering or leaving it, but there was a trail leading to the tent that was wide enough for a pickup truck, and, in fact, she'd noticed tire tracks. What had been delivered to that tent? There was another supply tent where foodstuffs were stored, along with medical supplies, but that tent was kept open. Why was this tent closed?

Kori slowly unzipped the entry to her own tent and peeked outside. Then she crawled out and, crouching behind the tent, gazed about the camp. Everything was still and quiet, though she could hear random snores and the sounds of the jungle from the trees beyond the clearing. She knew there were sentries in place, but she also knew they were at the very outer edges of the camp. The tent she wanted to examine was toward the middle of the camp and she knew that if she kept low, she'd remain out of sight.

Under the moonlight, she crawled along the ground navigating between tents and being careful not to get snagged in any tent's guy wire and cause it to collapse on its occupants.

Finally, she made it to the tent in question where she could see that the nylon door was zipped and secured with a combination lock. Simple enough. Kori placed her finger along the shackle part of the lock, applying pressure to it, and then began turning the dial clockwise until she felt a subtle tick of resistance in the shackle. The first number. She repeated the process going counterclockwise until she was able to determine the second number. Once she had those, she arrived at the third and final number by trial and error. The whole process took about five minutes and Kori was inside the tent.

In the darkness, she could make out a stack of oblong shapes. She hesitated using the light on her phone but had no choice. She hoped the thickness of the tent's walls would prevent any kind of glow from being visible from the outside. With the light, she saw that the shapes were long wooden crates, each about eight feet in length by two feet in width and around two feet high. There were three stacks of them and they were stacked three high. On one of the stacks, Kori could see that the lid of the topmost crate was loose and askew. The crates were slightly staggered and Kori was able to step up on the bottom one to pull herself up to see into the top crate. She slid the top off, reached inside, and brushed aside the straw that had been used as packing material. She almost gasped aloud at what she saw. She kept brushing away the straw, uncovering the contents of what had been loaded into the crates: weapons of every description. Seemingly every weapon used by the US Army—M500 shotguns, M14 rifles, M240 machine guns, sniper rifles, even grenade launchers.

All of it brand new.

Kori replaced the straw, slid the lid back over the crate, stepped down, and turned off her light. Then she crawled out of the tent, zipped up the opening, and put the padlock back in place. She crawled back to her tent and was just about inside when she heard a voice behind her.

"Strange time of night to be taking a walk, isn't it Ms. Bridges?"

She turned to see Oscar Rentería, flashlight in hand, a most serious look upon his face. How much had he seen? When did he first notice her?

"Yes, it certainly is," Kori replied smilingly, "but when nature calls, one has to answer, doesn't one?"

"Yes, of course, but it seems as though you were coming from the middle of the camp."

"Right? I tell ya, my sense of direction—I wouldn't give you two cents for it. I mean, I could get lost in a phone booth. And what are you doing up, Señor Vallejo? Can't sleep? Who can with all these strange jungle noises? Camping's not really my thing to begin with. I'm something of a city girl. My, my, I must say I don't know how you guys do it. It's admirable, what you're willing to do for your cause. And of course it's all going to go into the article, I can assure you of that."

Rentería said nothing and Kori knew he was sizing her up, trying to determine whether she was being truthful, wondering if something in her expression was going to give her away. Most likely, he hadn't seen where she'd been. He'd only seen her returning. She maintained her innocent smile.

Finally, Rentería forced a smile of his own and said, "Yes, it can be rough, but we will all sleep well after the success of the revolution. If you'll excuse me, Ms. Bridges, I'll let you get back to sleep. We will be returning you to your hotel first thing in the morning."

Rentería turned and walked away as Kori entered her tent and exhaled. She lay down on her cot but slept not a wink the rest of the night.

"I'm telling you, Chief, there was enough weaponry there for an entire army. Everything you can imagine. And all courtesy of the United States government."

Kori had called Eaglethorpe upon her return to Hotel San Benito. She had had coffee with Prieto and Rentería that morning, then a soldier drove her back in one of the pickup trucks. Rentería had said nothing over coffee about the middle-of-the-night encounter. At one point, Prieto had asked him when he'd be going back to San Benito for further reconnaissance and Rentería had replied "in a few days." The rest of the conversation revolved around the latest numbers as reported by the Ministry of Economics, all patently bogus, Prieto had declared. "Just more government propaganda to try to placate the people."

"It doesn't make sense, Kori," said Eaglethorpe. "Agent Foster has been checking his sources at the State Department. Of course, there's nothing official, but the US seems to be unequivocally backing Estrada's government, not Prieto's band of rebels. There's no reason why US weapons should be in the hands of Prieto."

"I know, Chief. And that's also what Alvin Reeves, the CIA agent in Rio, confirmed. In fact, we're supposedly sending weapons to Estrada. But somehow, they're ending up in Prieto's camp."

"Strange."

"Very. In the meantime, I plan on checking on something else, something pretty disturbing. Prieto mentioned that Estrada is developing sarin gas."

"Oh?"

"Yep. I have the address of where the plant is. I'll pay a visit and see if I can substantiate."

"So not only nuclear weapons, but poison gas."

"Apparently."

"That makes it even more important that we find out what's going on down there, Agent Briggs."

"Well, I have a hunch that the key is Oscar Rentería. That's the guy who has the answers."

"So how do you think he fits in exactly?"

"Well, my initial thoughts were that he was buddying up to Prieto for surveillance purposes. I figured he was reporting back to Estrada. But this shipment of arms changes things."

"You said he comes back to the city for reconnaissance."

"Right. That's where he supposedly was when I first showed up at the camp."

"Then you need to tail him when he comes back again."

"Negative, Chief. We can't take the chance of him spotting me. You should have seen the look on his face when he caught me out of my tent last night. He's already suspicious enough. Besides, say what you will about the CIA, but you have to admit they're at least a little harder to spy on than your everyday citizen."

"True. But someone's got to follow him. Who does he meet with when he comes back to the city? Where does he go? I could call Agent Vidal, but of course he's still recovering from the gunshot wound. Plus, Rentería has already met him. I suppose we could send Gibson down there."

"Can I make a suggestion?"

"Hmm . . . let me guess."

"She's the best, Chief."

"I thought you were the best."

"Well, next to me, I guess."

"What would be her cover? I know she speaks Spanish fluently, but she still has that Russian accent."

"Lots of Eastern Europeans have emigrated to Latin America. She could be visiting family. Really, Chief, we just need to get her past airport security. She'll keep a low profile once she's in the country. And I sure could use her help."

"Okay, Briggs. Who am I to argue? I'll have Cooper put something together for her. We'll have Anya Kovalev on the next plane."

13

— • —

Rampart Agent Anya Kovalev, based in Russia, flew from Moscow to Paris to Rio De Janeiro to San Benito in a little over twenty-two hours, including layovers.

"Could you not find a case to work on that was farther away, my American friend?" she asked Kori as the two sat in Kori's hotel room. They had met at the bar where Kori had introduced Anya to Santiago as one of the *Post*'s foreign correspondents. Then they'd ordered beers and taken them up to the room where they could talk freely.

"Sorry, my Russian friend, but I knew you'd never forgive me if I didn't include you in on this one. Haven't you always wanted to see a revolution up close and personal?"

"I was there when the Soviet Union fell, Kori."

"Well, true, but you must have been just a little girl. Besides, that was a fairly bloodless affair, Anya. This one could get really ugly."

"Yes, and who would want to miss *that*?"

"Oh, c'mon, it's going to be fun, you'll see. And besides, you can't beat the Hotel San Benito, huh?"

"Pure luxury."

"Wait until you see the city. Poverty, crime, gangs, prostitution—a little something for everyone!"

"Can't wait."

"So, let me tell you what's going on."

"Not so fast, my friend. As you can see, my glass is empty."

"So it is. Okay, I'll go back downstairs and get us a couple more beers."

"Thanks. And I'll wait here with the door locked so as to not become a robbery or kidnap victim."

"See? You've already got the spirit of the place!"

Kori returned with a couple more drafts and then filled Anya in on everything she had thus far uncovered.

"So one thing is unclear to me," said Anya. "Who is the US backing in this little drama?"

"Well, it depends on who you mean by 'US,'" Kori replied. "Officially, the US has no position. While you were en route, I made a stop at the US embassy and interviewed our Miranda ambassador. His answers to my questions about US policy in this country were maddeningly vacuous." Between her phone call with Eaglethorpe and Anya's arrival, Kori had visited the embassy as Kelly Bridges. The ambassador had agreed to see her but had remained carefully neutral, saying only that the State Department wanted what was best for the Mirandan people. "We are, of course, in favor of their ability to determine for themselves who their leader should be," he had said.

"Unofficially," Kori continued, "the CIA seems to be backing Estrada's regime. So does US oil. And quite possibly, Secretary of State Lloyd Higgins, although you wouldn't know it by the ambassador's statements. Then again, he might be completely in the dark about the secretary's position, which may, when all is said and done, reflect not the government's position at all, but his own personal—which is to say, financial—position. Meanwhile, however, CIA agent Oscar Rentería seems to be on the side of the rebels. I thought maybe he was acting as a sort of double agent to gain intel for Estrada, but it can't be a coincidence that he's in Prieto's camp along with a tent full of US military weapons."

"Yes, that part is confusing. This Rentería fellow is the key, it seems to me."

"I said the exact same thing to the chief."

"And what are your thoughts, Kori? About the whole political situation here? You've spent time with both sides. Who are the good guys?"

"The rebels, clearly. Anya, look around. This country is a mess. Estrada is a nut job."

"You like Prieto?"

"He speaks from the heart, Anya. He is the people's best hope."

"So you'd like to see a revolution?"

"Well, of course I was kidding about wanting to see a bloody one."

"I know."

"But, Anya, if there were a way for a peaceful transition of power from Estrada to Prieto, this country could be fixed."

"So you think we should help Prieto?"

"Yes. Yes, I do."

"But, Kori, you are a representative of Rampart. Rampart does not interfere with the inner politics of countries."

"I know all that, believe me. And it's all well and good—and easy as pie—to hold to theoretical ideals like that from a distance. But this is the real world here. We're talking about people's lives. I've seen it up close. Anya, if you saw a crime taking place, a robbery, let's say, and you knew you could stop it, wouldn't you?"

"Of course."

"Well, multiply that crime times 25 million, the population of Miranda, and how can you say that we should stay uninvolved?"

"But how do you know that Lucas Prieto can succeed? Not just with the revolution, but with whatever government he installs afterward?"

"It would be better than the government that's in power now."

"Do you know this for a fact?'

"Well—"

"And even if you are correct, would that be enough?"

"It would be a start. Look, we've got the ear of the executive branch. We could help Prieto. With the war *and* with the peace. The United States can help bring about the transition of power to a free and democratic government. We could ensure legitimate elections. We could help the Mirandans rewrite their constitution. We could—"

"Nation-build?"

"Well, I mean . . . "

"*That* always works. I cannot foresee any future problems there, my friend. History has always smiled upon American nation-building."

"Oh, Anya, I know what you're saying. I really do. But spend a few days here, spend some time talking to the people, spend some time listening to Prieto. And see if your feelings don't change."

"I have no doubt your feelings are in the right place, Kori. Of course they are. I would only remind you that our function is strictly intel, for the purposes of protecting the United States from foreign and domestic threats. Miranda's politics do not threaten the United States."

"Well, that may not be entirely true."

"The nuclear weapons."

"Right. Plus, there is the sarin gas that Estrada is developing."

"Weapons of mass destruction? Where have I heard that one before . . . "

"Anya, when did you become such a cynic?"

Anya chuckled. "Probably somewhere between Paris and Rio. It was a long flight, you know. Listen, my friend, I am merely playing devil's advocate with you. These are big issues and I would only suggest that we think very carefully about what we're going to report back to Rampart with, and what recommendations we're going to offer. Our reporting to HQ needs to be unbiased."

"I know, Anya. You're right, of course. I don't mean to get defensive. You're asking all the right questions, the same questions I would ask if you were recommending involvement in some Eastern European country."

"The world can be a confusing place, Kori. There is much gray area. We need to be careful."

"Indeed. And what we need more than anything else right now is better intel."

"Perhaps. And perhaps something else."

"What's that?"

"Dinner. I am starving."

The question over dinner at a café not far from the hotel was how best to put Anya on the trail of Oscar Rentería. The objective was clear enough: find out what his involvement was with Presidente Estrada. CIA agent Alvin Reeves in Rio had said that weapons were being sent to Estrada's army. So why were they sitting in the rebel camp? But somewhere over dessert, the plan became more ambitious.

"Kori," Anya had said, "we need to infiltrate the presidential palace. If Rentería is reporting to Estrada, he is no doubt meeting him there. That's where we need to be. We need to be a fly on the wall of those meetings. Somehow, we need to find a way into the palace."

Ambitious? Kori would have said audacious—just her kind of plan. The more audacious, the better. Which is why, right after dinner, the pair rode mopeds to the one location where Kori hoped they might find some help for their new scheme.

"Kelly!" said Lidia Amador, opening the door to her house and ushering Kori and Anya inside. "It is so nice to see you again."

"Thank you, Lidia. This is my friend Anya. She is visiting family."

"Very nice to meet you, Anya. Would you two like some coffee?"

"That would be very kind of you," said Kori, "if it's not too much trouble."

Coming out from the back bedroom at that moment was Pablo Amador, a grave expression on his face. He stared daggers at Kori, maintaining his stare as he said, "Yes, Lidia, please go into the kitchen and make some coffee for our guests."

"I'll only be a moment," Lidia said.

"Take your time, my dear. I will entertain."

When Lidia was out of earshot, Kori lowered her voice and said, "Look, Señor Amador, I am sorry to come here. I know what you said. I know you are concerned about my being found out and possibly jeopardizing you and your wife. I am sorry to break my promise by visiting you at your home, but I can assure you that my fellow agent and I were extraordinarily careful. Nobody followed us here from the city. Twice along the way, we rode off onto side streets and stopped and waited for any pursuer. There were none. Trust me. We do this for a living. The fact is, we need your help, Señor Amador."

Amador's expression softened. "I am listening."

"Gracias. Now, you mentioned the other night that you knew the CIA was supporting Presidente Estrada."

"*Sí.*"

"We are not so certain. Without going into detail, we have reason to believe that the CIA might now be backing the rebels."

Amador arched his eyebrows.

"But we need to know for sure," Kori continued.

"I must ask," Amador said, "whose side are you on?"

Kori glanced at Anya. "We are neutral," she said. "As I had mentioned, our job is to gather information. What my government does with that information is out of our control. I can tell you nothing about our organization, other than it reports to the president of the United States. That's where decisions ultimately get made. My colleague here has reminded me that we need to remain unbiased. That being said, I have to tell you, off the record, that based on what I have observed thus far, my heart is with *El Principio.*"

"Señora Bridges!" Lidia Amador, coming in from the kitchen with a tray of steaming coffee cups, was aghast. "Pablo," she said. "What in heaven's name are you discussing?"

Amador was quiet for a moment. Finally, he said, "These ladies are with a US intelligence agency, my dear. But not the CIA. An independent one. That is what you said the other night, yes . . . Kori, is it?" Kori nodded. "You are my wife, Lidia. You may as well know the truth. These women are here on a fact-finding mission. They have sought my help, and I am planning to oblige. It might be possible that the American government is now helping to support the rebels. As far as I am concerned, this would come as good news."

"Pablo! Just whispering such things . . ."

"I know, *mi querida*. But I have seen too much. I am weary. Presidente Estrada is driving this nation into the ground. And worse. I have not told you half of what I have seen. I am ashamed to say that I have been content watching it happen, safe in my *Policia Nacional* uniform. But perhaps these agents have come into our lives for a reason. Perhaps it is time for me to do something. Perhaps my duty is now to my country, not to its current leader."

"I'm sorry, Lidia," Kori said. "I wish I could have told you who I was when I first met you. But my interest was always in protecting you and your husband; I am well aware of how dangerous things can be. If it's not too late for proper introductions, my name is Kori Briggs and this is my associate Anya Kovalev."

Lidia nodded almost involuntarily, mouth hanging open, trying to take it all in. "So you are not Roberto's sister-in-law?" she asked at last.

Kori hesitated, torn between revealing too much and opening up to gain Lidia's trust. "Roberto is a fellow agent," she said at last.

"Oh, my," Lidia said. Then she crossed herself and absent-mindedly sat the tray down on the coffee table.

For Lidia's sake, Anya sensed it would be a good idea to bring some normalcy and convention into the room. "That coffee sure smells good," she warmly smiled.

Lidia gathered herself. "Oh, yes, of course. I'm so sorry. Here you are." She handed cups and saucers to everyone and Pablo suggested they all take a seat.

"What can I do to help, Señorita Briggs?" he asked.

"We need access to the presidential palace. You said you have purposely been taking assignments away from the action, patrolling remote barrios. Can you ask to be reassigned? Can you get close to the palace?"

"Perhaps. But what do you want to do there?"

"We want to sneak in and set up some surveillance in Estrada's office."

"That is bold, Señorita Briggs. And perilous."

"We know. But we also think it's necessary. Our plan is to listen in on Estrada's next conversations with a CIA operative named Oscar Rentería. We know that Estrada doesn't leave the palace, so we believe any meetings with Rentería will most likely take place in the presidential office."

"That is true. It is Estrada's refuge. But how do you plan on sneaking in?"

"That's where we need your help. There must be a way you can get us in there. Or, I should say, get Anya in there. Estrada knows me."

"I will pose as a member of the servant staff," Anya added. "Surely he does not know them all."

"It would not matter if he did," said Amador. "There is much turnover on the staff. Your plan is plausible. But I do not see how I can get you in. The security is extremely tight, and more so lately."

"I know," said Kori. "I experienced it firsthand when I went there and pretended to be a *Post* reporter. At least at the front gate. But there must be various entrances to the palace, yes? All we need is a back door or window. We need someone on the inside to leave something unlocked somewhere. Anything. Any point of entry will suffice. I know the layout of the place, or at least how to get to Estrada's office. I'll give Anya instructions and she'll be able to sneak in and plant a few bugs, all the while assuming the role of someone on the housekeeping staff."

"There are security cameras throughout."

"Well," said Kori, "then we need someone on the inside who can at least temporarily disable any camera that might be focused on our point of entry. Once Anya is in, she'll blend in as just another staff member. As far as planting the bugs—"

"Do not worry about that," Anya said. "I can do that, how do you say? on the sly, while I am doing something as simple and innocent-looking as dusting a lamp."

"There are guards in Estrada's office," said Amador.

"They will not notice my sleight of hand."

"Where did you get the bugs?"

Truthfully, the bugs were standard issue Rampart equipment. Kori had all the tools of the trade in what looked like a makeup travel kit. She kept the wiretaps in lipstick tubes. "Sorry, I'm afraid that's classified," she said.

"Of course."

"So what do you think, Señor Amador? Can you help us? *Will* you help us?"

Pablo glanced at his wife who sat nervously but said nothing. "Lidia, my dear," he said. "I will do nothing unless you agree to it."

Lidia sighed deeply. "I love our country, Pablo," she said. "It has been good to us. But I know there has been a cost. I am not blind. I see the suffering. I know this country is not like it used to be. I remember when Estrada took power. I remember the promise of a rebirth for this land. It has been sad to see that promise wither and die. And I know you are unhappy, my husband, and it pains me to see you this way. You need to do what is right. That's the kind of man I married. That's the man I fell in love with."

Pablo smiled. "Señorita Briggs, Señorita Kovalev, I will find a way for you. I will go into the station tomorrow morning and ask for a reassignment. I will not be turned down. The desk sergeant owes me a favor. I covered for him one day when he was too hungover to come into work. Give me until tomorrow afternoon. I will call you then."

"Thank you, Señor Amador," said Kori. "We are not unaware of the risk you are taking. And we will do all we can to mitigate it, to keep you safe and above suspicion. You have our word. Thank you. Thank you both."

14

From her hotel room the next morning, Kori decided to check in with her mother and ask about the date with Bertram.

"It was lovely, dear," Joan said. "Just lovely."

"That's great to hear, Mom. And how was the Denzel movie?"

"Denzel was wonderful as always. Afterward, Bertram and I went for coffee and we had a long chat. I feel so bad for him."

"How come?"

"He's going through such a hard time. First of all, there's that problem with his former business partner. My, that man must be a complete crook. Bertram's finances are still all tied up. And then, as if that state of affairs isn't bad enough, he has a sister who's apparently in very poor health."

"Oh, I'm sorry to hear that, Mom."

"Yes, she needs a kidney transplant."

"Wow, that's tough."

"Yes. And the problem is that she has no health insurance. Bertram wants to pay for the transplant, of course, but he's having trouble getting his finances squared away. Oh, Kori, if you had heard him describing the situation to me. He was so sad. I thought he was going to cry."

Were those more alarms Kori heard? "So, Mom, where does this sister of his live? Maybe you could go visit her with Bertram."

"Unfortunately, she lives in California. Sacramento, to be exact. That's where Bertram is originally from."

"Is she married? Does she have any other family?"

"Nope, just Bertram. He said they're a couple of years apart, but they grew up just like twins. They're very close. Apparently, they survived a terrible childhood together."

"Uh-huh."

"When they were little, their parents were both killed in a tragic car accident. They went to live with an aunt and uncle who were dirt poor and who were awful to them. They were always hungry and the uncle used to beat them. Can you imagine?"

"Terrible."

"Bertram managed to get away after high school, coming east where he attended Georgetown on a lacrosse scholarship. Then, after bouncing around in different jobs, he got into the real estate business where he made his fortune and put his childhood behind him. But his sister stayed behind. She never was able to really make anything of herself. Truthfully, I think Bertram feels guilty about it. Isn't that heartbreaking?"

"Yep, it sure is. Listen, Mom, Bertram hasn't, like, you know, asked you for any financial help for his sister, has he?"

"Oh, my no, Kori. He's a wealthy man. He doesn't need my help. He's just not very liquid right now. But once he gains access to his money again, he'll be fine. More than fine, I'm sure."

"Right, and what was the deal with that again, Mom?"

"Well, apparently he had a security issue. Somehow his old business partner was able to gain access to his primary bank account. So, he had to close that account, open a new one, and now he's having to move some money around to fund the new account. Oh, he explained it all. It's all very complicated, but evidently most of his money is tied up in long-term securities and it takes time to cash them out. The money that's not tied up in real estate, that is. Naturally, that's where his real fortune is, but that's even less liquid, of course."

"Uh-huh."

"And besides, asking anyone for money is just not the way Bertram is at all. He's a very proud man. In fact, he made it clear to me when I offered to help—"

"You offered to help?"

"Well, of course, Kori. I'm not made of stone, you know. His sister's story is just so sad."

"And what did Bertram say when you offered to help?"

"He thanked me but said he'd find a way to work it out. And I have no doubt that he will. He's a very smart man. Very savvy. And he's got the best attorneys and financial advisors."

"When are you seeing him again, Mom?"

"We're going for a drive tomorrow to Brookside Gardens, and then lunch at a nice place he knows around there. Oh, but enough about me and Bertram. I've been going on and on. Tell me, dear, what have you been up to?"

Kori talked about Italy, then mentioned that she'd be flying home the next day, but stopping first in New York to meet with the Brooklyn branch of Gladstone Conveyor. "We have a new manager there," she explained. At least now she'd ostensibly be in the same time zone and wouldn't have to be so careful about timing her calls. But the Bertram thing bothered her. Joan was an intelligent woman, but a trusting person and a sucker for a hard-luck story. Maybe Bertram's story was true, but it seemed a little fishy to Kori.

Eventually, the two hung up and Kori forced herself to switch gears and focus again on the problems of Miranda. Pablo Amador had promised to call Kori and Anya that afternoon with news of his reassignment to the palace. That left the morning free and the two agents decided to use the time to ride their mopeds to the address Prieto had given Kori, the warehouse used by the Ministry of Science for, allegedly, the production of sarin gas. Kori had contacted Agent Cooper in DC for a satellite shot of the building, which he had subsequently texted her.

The huge warehouse was about thirty minutes south of the city on a main road. Kori and Anya found themselves riding through an industrial area, past oil and gas facilities, and small manufacturing and machinery plants, many of which were closed, their windows boarded up or broken.

The warehouse in question, on the left side of the road, was large and, in contrast to the other buildings in the area, pristine, with freshly painted block that gave way to shiny metal walls. As promised by Prieto, it was heavily guarded. The agents noted the fortified main gate complete with guardhouse and security bollards. The Mirandan flag waved over the entrance. There was no name on the building, however. Not that Kori expected to see a big sign reading, "Sarin Gas Plant." But the building had all the markings of a governmental facility. They drove past and pulled over a couple of hundred yards farther down the road.

"So?" said Kori. "What do you think?"

"Well, it is certainly an imposing building. It seems as if something important is going on in there."

"Like the manufacturing of deadly nerve gas?"

"We don't know that for sure."

"True. But what else could it be?"

"Who knows? It could be a lot of things."

"I'll bet you dinner it's sarin gas."

"You're on, my friend. But the problem is one of verification."

"That's not such a big problem. We go in, take a look around, make our determination, and get out."

"Well, when you put it like that, yes, it does seem pretty easy. But just how, pray tell, do you plan on getting us in?"

"There's got to be an entrance that's easier to access than the main gate. I've seen buildings like this before, Anya. They make a big show of security on the side that's facing the street, which scares most people away, and then they completely ignore other points of entry. It's a big building. Probably a hundred thousand square feet, right?"

"Probably."

"Then I'll bet there's a way in somewhere. There's got to be."

"But where?"

"Well, from Cooper's satellite shot, it seems as if the rear of the building backs up to a pretty densely wooded area. And it looks like there's a street on the other side of that that runs parallel with this one." She looked down the road. "There. That intersection up ahead. If we hang a left there, we'll come to it. We can take it up to the woods, park our bikes, and hike through the woods to the back of the building."

"Okay. Sounds like a plan to me. Let's go."

Minutes later, they were on the parallel road, narrow and rutted and obviously not made with mopeds in mind, but at least empty of traffic. They came up even with the back of the building where a thicket of trees and heavy vegetation stretched about fifty yards between the rear of the building and the road, just as it showed on Cooper's satellite photo. The agents pulled their bikes over and walked them into the thicket where they laid them down, out of sight from anybody who might drive by.

"Come on," said Kori, and the two began trudging through the dense brush, angling their way between crowded banana plants, ferns, dwarf palms, and bamboo, all darkly shaded by rubber, kapok, and balsa trees.

"I feel as though we ought to be using machetes to hack our way through this," Anya remarked.

"Just watch out for snakes."

"Snakes?"

"Sure."

"As if the mosquitos are not bad enough."

Fifty yards seemed like a hundred to the agents, but they finally came out of the other side of the thicket to the rear of the building.

"I think I need a shower," said Kori. "But look, Anya, what did I tell you?"

A tall, chain-link fence separated the woods from the building. The back of the building had a dozen truck docks, all empty, accessed from the pavement that ran between the fence and the building, a distance of about a hundred feet.

"The fence doesn't even have barbed wire," Kori continued, "and check out the third dock from the left. The rollup door isn't even closed all the way. We can crawl underneath it."

"It doesn't make sense," said Anya. "There aren't even any guards around this side of the building."

"Sure it makes sense. They're not expecting anybody to come in this way. You can't even see the back of the building from the road. Who else besides us would take that hike?"

"I don't know, Kori. Something seems off. There's nobody back here at all. And why no trucks backed up to the docks?"

"Who knows? But there's only one way to find out what's going on. Feel like a climb?"

"Sure, why not?"

The agents scaled the twelve-foot-high fence, pulling themselves up and over it, lowering themselves part way down the other side, and then dropping to the ground.

"That would have been impossible with barbed wire," said Anya. "We would have been sliced and diced."

"That's the truth," said Kori. "Race you to the open loading dock."

"You're on," said Anya.

The two stayed low and ran across the pavement to the dock. Then they crouched down behind the four-foot-high dock wall. There was about two feet of open space between the rollup door and the dock. They drew themselves up and peered inside the building.

"I don't see anybody," whispered Kori. "Let's sneak in."

They pulled themselves up to the dock and crawled into the building. Then they rose to their knees and looked around.

"Now it makes sense," said Anya. "Now I can see why nobody is guarding this place back here."

"Indeed," said Kori, rising to her feet, dumbfounded at the sight before her.

There were just enough lights hanging from the tall ceiling of the warehouse to reveal a building that was completely and utterly empty.

"There's nothing here," said Kori. "Not a single table or desk or shelf. A hundred thousand square feet of nothing. Not even any people."

"Just the personnel in the guardhouse out front," Anya said. "But guarding what?"

"How strange. What do you make of it?"

"I'll tell you what I make of it," Anya replied. "I think someone owes me dinner, my friend. That's what I make of it."

15

In Kori's room at the Hotel San Benito, Anya sat on the bed while Kori paced and briefed Eaglethorpe by phone.

"That's right, Chief, empty. But you should have seen the guard house. Someone is certainly intent on making it look as if something big and important is going on in that building."

"A bluff?" offered Eaglethorpe.

"It would seem so. But, Chief, Prieto mentioned that he had spies within the government. That's how he learned about the presumed sarin gas in the first place. But they must not be very good spies. Or at least not very thorough in their surveillance."

"Or maybe they're double agents, Kori."

"Yes, Chief, I'll bet you're right. Estrada set up a fake poison gas plant and then had the 'spies' report back to Prieto. I'm sure Prieto's own men checked things out and saw the same façade that we saw. Apparently it didn't occur to them to hike through the thicket of jungle around back like we did to confirm that the plant was actually operating."

"Nobody's as thorough as you, Agent Briggs."

"Thanks, Chief."

"Estrada's thinking must be that having the rebels believe he has the capability of launching sarin gas at them is as good as actually having it. Perception is reality."

"So they say."

"Makes you wonder about the nuclear weapons."

"Right, I hadn't even thought of that!"

"We know they're big importers of uranium. That's no secret. It's been confirmed by a lot of intelligence agencies around the world. But it's a big step from there to weapons-grade nuclear material. A big step technologically, and a big step financially."

"My police contact was pretty sure they've taken those steps, but I don't think he's seen it firsthand. We'll do a little more digging on that front."

"Good plan."

"In the meantime, we're waiting on that same contact to call. He's agreed to get Anya into the presidential palace."

"That's excellent, Briggs. Good work. Do me a favor and tell her to be careful, would you? Can you imagine what would happen to her if she were to be found out?"

"I can imagine it, and I'm pretty sure Agent Kovalev has imagined it, too. Don't worry, Chief. I'm sure she'll stay on her toes."

"Then call me when you have more information."

"Will do."

They hung up and Kori turned to Anya. "Chief wants you to be careful."

Anya smiled. "He's a good guy, isn't he?"

"Yeah, the chief's the best."

Kori was certain that Anya had, indeed, imagined what would happen to her if the people in the palace discovered she was an intruder. But if she felt any apprehension, she sure wasn't showing it.

In fact, she turned to Kori and spoke casually as if she hadn't a care in the world. "So, Kori," she said, "what is new with you? We haven't had a chance to really chat since I got here."

Kori was grateful for conversation that didn't focus on the dangers ahead of them. "Not much, my friend," she replied, sitting down in the room's only chair. "I was enjoying a nice Italian vacation before the chief sent me here. In Mantua, to be exact. I was headed to Verona when duty called, as duty always seems to."

"Duty is a bitch, no?"

"Duty is a bitch," Kori nodded.

"And who were you with in Mantua?"

"Nobody. Just me, Anya. Sometimes I prefer it that way."

"I understand."

"And you? How is Nikolai?

"He is fine. We are still talking about marriage, but nothing has been decided."

"I see. And who's responsible for that?"

"Me, I guess. I am the one doing the foot-dragging."

"Still not convinced that a marriage can work between a civilian and a Rampart agent?"

"Yes. It seems to me that it is too much to keep such a big secret from a spouse."

"Other Rampart agents do it."

"Perhaps. I suppose I am not very good at lying."

"Well, you'd better be," Kori chuckled. "Hopefully, to-morrow you'll have to lie your way around the presidential palace."

"Ah, but you see, that is different. That is play-acting. And I do not care about the people who are being fooled. A marriage is another thing. It is a sacred trust, is it not?"

"I suppose so."

"I do not want to fool my husband on a daily basis."

"Yes, but you're fooling him now, right? He thinks you work for the Russian Commerce Agency, sent abroad to procure business for Russia."

"Yes, and I have been thinking lately, that it is just as bad to lie to a boyfriend as it is to lie to a husband."

"So what are you going to do? Obviously, you can't come clean. You swore an oath, just like the rest of us."

"Of course. I would never divulge my involvement with Rampart."

Kori looked alarmed. "Anya, you're not going to *quit* Rampart, are you?"

"Never. It is my—how do you say?—life's blood."

"Thank God. We need you."

"Thank you, my friend."

"Well, if you're not going to quit and you're not going to divulge your role with Rampart, then I don't see how . . . Oh, Anya, you're thinking of breaking up with Nikolai, aren't you?"

"Maybe," Anya said, casting her eyes downward.

"Wow. How long have you been thinking that?"

"A few weeks now."

"Do you still . . . do you still love him, Anya?"

"Of course. Very much."

"Cripes, I don't know what to say. This must be a lot for you to be carrying around. I wish I had some kind of wise advice, but you know my track record with long-term relationships."

"There is nothing to say, my friend, and no advice you can offer. It's just something I need to work out for myself." Anya smiled. "I thank you for listening, Kori."

"Sure. Anytime."

"Is that your phone buzzing?"

"Ah, yes!" Kori dug into her purse and retrieved her phone. "Briggs here . . . Señor Amador! We have been awaiting your call."

The staff entrance to the presidential palace was in the back. It was not, however, any less secure than the front entrance. There were the same sets of metal detectors, body scanners, and vigilant security officers scrutinizing the IDs of all who entered, even upper-level staff members. Pablo Amador, having been granted his request to spend a few days on presidential guard duty, decided that a better way in was a little-used side door at the end of a remote hallway on the ground floor of the palace where there were some storage rooms, a large mechanical room with water heaters and HVAC equipment, and a room with janitorial supplies. It was the least-visited hallway in the palace, a narrow corridor with low lighting from fluorescent tubes running along the ceiling. Nobody had even thought to place security cameras down there. When the side door was used at all, it was to bring in equipment or tools. More than once, it had been left unlocked by careless maintenance workers, meaning no suspicions would be raised if Amador were to stray down there and unlock it himself.

A camera was trained on the exterior of the door, but Amador believed if, after unlocking the door, he went around and escorted Anya in through the door—him, a loyal, twenty-year veteran of *Policia Nacional*, and her, dressed in the janitorial uniform of the palace maintenance staff—the officers monitoring the cameras in the main security office wouldn't even look twice. Besides, in all, there were probably fifty cameras in operation throughout the palace, meaning fifty screens that were being watched at the same time by typically no more than two men.

All this was being discussed between Kori and Anya and Pablo Amador at his home. After his phone call to Kori, they had decided to meet again that evening, with Kori and Anya once again making certain nobody had followed them. Lidia made dinner and Pablo opened a bottle of wine.

"Lidia worked in the palace at one time," Amador said. "She's about your size, Señorita Kovalev. I'm sure her uniform will fit you. And they never change uniforms. Lidia, will you fetch it, please? Now, here is an official laminated palace staff ID and lanyard. I swiped it at the station this afternoon when nobody was looking. It will work if nobody inspects it too closely."

"Marta Reynoso," Anya said, reading the ID.

"She had maid duties. She'd just started working at the palace when she took ill. Now she's on leave and she had to turn in her ID. Nobody really had a chance to know her, so I think you'll be okay."

"She has dark hair."

"You should probably have dark hair too."

"Anya," Kori smiled, "haven't you always wanted to be a brunette?"

"Not really. Haven't you heard? Blonds have more fun."

"Debatable."

"The problem," Amador continued, "is the date on the ID."

"A month ago," said Anya.

"Correct. That is why you cannot allow it to be scrutinized."

"If we had more time," Kori said, "I'd have our Agent Cooper send a forged ID that I guarantee would be foolproof. He's something of a master."

"Yes, but even if time was not a factor," said Amador, "the mail here is routinely inspected, especially mail from out of the country. And besides, if there is any suspicion, the guard may also ask to see a secondary ID, her national identification card. I am sorry, Señorita Kovalev. It is the best I could do. We can only hope you do not get stopped on the grounds and questioned."

"I am not worried," said Anya.

Lidia came into the room just then with a uniform of the janitorial staff of the presidential palace. It was on a hanger and she held it aloft.

"Pretty ordinary," said Kori. "I've heard about Estrada's womanizing. I was half-expecting some kind of sexy French maid number."

"Me too," said Anya. "This is somewhat of a relief."

Kori chuckled. "You were concerned about the style of uniform, but you're not concerned about getting stopped by a guard?"

"In a sexy French maid uniform, I might be more likely to get stopped," Anya smiled.

"True enough." Kori turned to Amador. "Can you review the plan for us again, Señor Amador?"

"Of course. At around three o'clock tomorrow afternoon, I will open that side door. Nobody will be down there then. That is a break time. Señorita Kovalev, I will text you once the door is unlocked. You will go to the back staff entrance. I will be there. You will enter the security area and, before anybody can look too closely at your ID, well, Señorita Briggs, that's where you come in."

"Don't worry about me," said Kori. "If causing a distraction is a problem, then we're not going to have a problem."

"Good," said Amador. "Then, Señorita Kovalev, in the confusion created by Señorita Briggs, I will usher you out of the side door of the security area, allowing us to avoid the room beyond where the metal detectors are. There are additional guards back there, but it is a different room and they do not have a good view of the very front entryway. They will not see us exit, but the door we go out of will conveniently put us inside the perimeter of the fence and onto the grounds of the palace."

Out of the corner of her eye, Kori noticed Lidia crossing herself.

"Then," Amador went on, "we will simply walk around the side of the building toward the unlocked door. We will walk with purpose, but not too fast. It will look to the security cameras as though I am simply escorting a staff maid to the door that leads to the janitorial supply room."

"Yes, but from the outside," said Kori. "Won't that look suspicious? And in through a door that's supposed to be locked, right?"

"It is not a perfect plan," said Amador. "But it is not as if we will be dressed like the rebels. Or even civilians. We will be dressed as if we belong there. The unlocked door will escape scrutiny because we will not be sneaking up to it. We will laugh and smile. Knowing some of the other members of the presidential security staff, I can assume they may even believe I am escorting the maid to a private area of the palace for a romantic tryst." Amador looked over at Lidia. "Forgive me, my wife," he smiled.

"You are forgiven, my dear."

Looking back toward Anya, he added, "But once you're in, Señorita Kovalev, you are on your own."

"I understand, Señor Amador," said Anya. "Getting me in is all we need. I can make it to the president's office from there, plant the devices, and get out."

"Yes, and getting out is easy. You'll simply walk through the rear security area where you came in and out the back gate. They will check to make sure you are not taking anything from the palace, but they do not check IDs of people who are exiting. Once you're through the gate, you will be home safe."

"In the meantime," said Kori, "I'll set up shop down the street. There is a small, abandoned store two blocks away, easily within range of the bugs. I'll set up the receiver there, and we'll be able to monitor every conversation that takes place in the presidential office."

"Excellent," said Amador.

"You know, I have a very good feeling about this. I think it'll all go off without a hitch."

"Yes, what is that expression you always use?" said Anya. "Easy-peasy."

"Yep, Easy-peasy."

Amador smiled and lifted his wine glass. "Easy-peasy," he said, and they all touched glasses. Lidia joined in but then sat her glass down and crossed herself once again.

16

—·—

As anticipated, nobody was around the next day when Officer Pablo Amador wandered through the remote hallway on the ground floor of the palace and unlocked the side door. Then he texted Anya: *Good to go.* Then he deleted the text.

A few minutes later, he strolled into the outer office of the staff security entrance. "Gentlemen," he said to the two uniformed officers at their desks, "I have been told that we need to be on the lookout for this woman." He pulled out a photograph of Kori and passed it to them. "Her name is Kelly Bridges and she is from an American newspaper. Presidente Estrada does not want to meet with her, but we believe she will nevertheless try to make an attempt to enter for an interview. Probably through the front gate, but if that doesn't work, she will most likely try to come in through here. She is supposedly very determined. No matter what story she gives, she is to be sent away."

"Why are you telling us this, Pablo?" one of the guards asked. "If she is not on the guest list, she will be denied entry regardless of what she says."

"You would think so," said Amador. "But somehow she got in the other day without an appointment. Apparently, Colonel Tovar let her in. Now, the president has expressly ordered that she be escorted off the property. Unharmed, of course."

At that moment, a woman with dark hair and sunglasses and dressed in the official servant's uniform of the presidential palace came into the security entrance, an official palace staff ID hanging around her neck on a lanyard.

"*Buen dia*," she said.

One of the guards rose from his desk to check the woman's ID but as he did so, Kelly Bridges of the *Washington Post* stormed into the office. She elbowed the servant out of the way and, staring straight ahead, attempted to walk past the guards.

"Whoa!" said the guard who had just stood up, placing himself directly in Kori's path and raising his hand. "You cannot come in here, señorita! You are not on the guest list."

"Nonsense!" Kori said. "Do you know who I am? I am a reporter from the United States and I am supposed to interview Presidente Estrada! I was promised an interview and I am not leaving here until I get one!"

"We cannot let you in!"

"That's what they said at the front gate. You know what I say? Bullshit! I am not going to take no for an answer. The world wants to know what Presidente Estrada is up to!"

Kori tried to sidestep the guard, which brought the other guard to his feet. Now they were both trying to corral her as she made left and right feints to get past them.

"We know who you are," said one of the guards, "and the president does not want to see you. He sent specific orders to us."

"Of course he wants to see me!" said Kori. "There's no way those orders came from him. Probably from some lower-level loser. Let's ask Presidente Estrada himself. Go ahead. Ask him! I'll bet you a hundred Mirandan dollars that the president would welcome me with open arms."

"We do not need to ask him. He is a busy man. Now, do not make us arrest you. You must leave and you must leave now."

Kori made one last evasive maneuver before each guard grabbed hold of an arm and the two spun her around and began shoving her back toward the door.

"Okay, okay, I'm going," she said in exasperation. "You don't need to push. I'll have you know I've been thrown out of better places than this! You haven't heard the last of me! I'll be back!"

As Kori made her way through the door, she glanced back over her shoulder to see that nobody else was in the security entryway. Anya and Amador were gone.

"The maintenance elevator is to the right," Amador said to Anya. "Do you have any questions?"

"Nope."

"Good luck."

"Thank you, Señor Amador."

Per the plan, the pair had strolled to the side door, chatting amiably, like coworkers going about their work. Inside, they'd found the hallway empty.

Amador took a left out of the hallway and Anya took a right, pushing a janitor cart she'd found in the janitorial storeroom. She made her way to the elevator and rode it up a floor. Then she exited the elevator and wheeled the cart down the long hallway toward the president's office. Chief of Staff Colonel Tovar was sitting at his desk in the anteroom. Anya looked down toward the floor and continued on, rolling the cart past him.

"Just a moment," Tovar said, getting up from his desk. "A maid was just in the president's office this morning to clean and vacuum. Why are you here now?"

Anya continued looking down. "I don't know, sir. They sent me."

"Who sent you?" he said, coming closer to her.

"Housekeeping, sir."

"Cortez?"

"*Sí.*"

"He always checks with me before allowing anybody access to the president's office."

"I was just told to come here, Sir."

"You know, I don't recall seeing you here before." He was standing right in front of her now.

"I'm new, Sir."

"Uh-huh. Let me see your ID."

Anya had twisted the lanyard so that only the back of the ID was visible. Now she had no choice but to show him the front. As she reached down for it, plotting her next move, the phone on Tovar's desk rang.

"One second," he said to her. Then he retreated to his desk. "Yes? . . . The meeting with the general?" Tovar looked down at his watch and winced. "I'm very sorry. It had completely slipped my mind . . . Yes, I am on my way; please apologize to the general for me." He hung up his phone, grabbed a file off his desk, and began sprinting down the hallway, the matter with the new maid completely forgotten.

Anya breathed a sigh of relief and wheeled the cart into the presidential office. Two inattentive guards were chatting with each other and leaning against the side wall. They glanced up at Anya as she came in, and then continued their conversation. Presidente Estrada was out, thus explaining the casual nature of the guards, and besides them, there was nobody else around.

She made her way to the far end of the office, passing a duster over Estrada's expansive desk, pausing at the antique, double-brass candelabra lamp. In a flash, she reached up into the black parchment shade and inserted one of the listening devices. Then she moved toward the center of the room and began dusting the coffee table that rested between the set of posh chairs. She pretended to drop her duster and bent down for it, slipping another listening device under the table. Eventually, she moved to the side of the office that was opposite the chatting guards and planted one final device in a potted bamboo palm. Three bugs, more or less equidistant from each other and collectively able to cover the entire office.

As she turned to head toward the door, she noticed the guards snap to attention, eyes staring straight ahead, bodies stock-still, as if they had always been that way.

Presidente Alonso Estrada had entered the room.

Anya stopped her cart and cast her eyes toward the floor in feigned deference. It would not be proper to continue until the president passed her. Only Estrada didn't pass her. He stopped in front of her.

"Well," he smiled. "I don't remember seeing you before, my dear."

She kept her eyes on the floor. "Yes Sir, I'm new, Sir."

"And what's your name, my dear?" Fortunately, he paid no attention to her ID.

"Marta Reynoso, Sir."

"What a lovely name. A lovely name for a lovely woman." He reached out and placed his hand under her chin and lifted her head. His smile was bigger now. "And what beautiful eyes you have. I must compliment Cortez. Frankly, some of the housekeepers he has hired have not been, shall we say, up to standard. Tell me, Marta, are they treating you all right?"

"Oh, yes, sir. Very much so."

"Excellent. And what kind of hours does Cortez have you working?"

"Until five o'clock, sir."

"I see. That is not long from now. I'll tell you what, Marta. Why don't you come back here after five? You can attend to my office again. It is very important to me that it be kept especially clean. It is the presidential office, after all. It is the most important office in the whole of Miranda, wouldn't you agree?"

"Oh, yes, sir."

"Do not worry; I will make sure you get paid overtime. Perhaps even a bonus on top of that. When you return, we can discuss your permanent assignment to my office."

"Permanent assignment, Sir?"

"Yes, we'll chat about it over a drink, Marta. Would you like that? Would you like to share a drink with your presidente?"

"Oh, yes, sir."

"Very good. Then I will see you at five, my dear." He took her hand and brought it up to his lips and kissed it.

Anya smiled. "Yes, Sir." Then she bowed her head and wheeled her cart out of the office, suddenly feeling as if she needed to take a very long, very hot shower. *Ick*, she thought.

With relief, she saw that Tovar hadn't made it back to his desk yet and she continued down the long hallway to the maintenance elevator. Down on the first floor, she ditched the cart and made her way toward the rear corridor that would lead her out the staff entrance. Before entering the security area, she glanced to her right to see an office where two guards appeared to be interrogating someone. The unfortunate person was in a chair, hands clasped behind him. The interrogators were standing over him, backs to the door. One was leaning down, his face right up to the face of his subject, tersely speaking to him. Anya slowed, trying unsuccessfully to make out what was being said. Then the interrogator rose to his full height and stepped to the side and Anya could make out the face of the person being questioned, realizing, to her horror, that it was none other than the face of Pablo Amador.

17

—·—

The windows of the abandoned shop were boarded up, the inside concealed from the street. From the look of the empty racks and some faded advertising posters stuck on the walls, it had apparently once been a clothing store. Kori had picked the lock of the back door and was now sitting on a chair in the darkened store, fiddling with a radio-like device on a table in front of her. Anya came bursting in through the back door.

"They got him," she said breathlessly.

"What?"

"They got Señor Amador. I saw him being interrogated on my way out."

"Crap. What happened?"

"I do not know, Kori. Everything went according to plan. He got me in, I accessed the presidential office, planted the bugs, and got out. But on my way to the staff exit, I saw Amador in a private security office. Two officers appeared to be giving him the third degree."

"But nobody caught you? Or questioned you?"

"No. Tovar seemed suspicious, but he was called away. I met Estrada himself, but he was far from suspicious. To tell the truth, he seemed enamored. I think I have a date with him this evening."

"Hey, good for you, Anya. Maybe if you play your cards right, you can be First Lady of a banana republic."

"Yes, every girl's dream, right? But, Kori, outside of those two, I had no interactions. I was in and I was out."

"They had Amador, but nobody questioned you when you left?"

"No. It was as he said it would be. They look you over quickly to make sure you're not pilfering anything, but they do not pay any attention to identification."

"Then they haven't connected Amador to you."

"Not yet, Kori. But remember what Amador said. It was not a perfect plan. If he has come under suspicion for whatever reason, they will roll the security tapes to track his movements for the day. They will see him letting me in the side door of the palace."

"Then they'll track your movements."

"And they will be able to determine that I accessed the presidential office."

"And they'll wonder what you were doing in there."

"And they'll sweep the place for bugs."

"Yep. Damn."

The two were silent for a moment. Finally, Anya said, "But Kori, we are being far too pessimistic. Think about it. I am sure Amador interacts with many people throughout the palace in his daily duties. He is known there. In fact, as I came into the security area, I overheard one of the guards call him by his first name. If they examine the tapes, I am sure they will see him with several people, not just me. Will anybody bother to pay attention to a lowly housekeeper's movements, just because one of the palace officers walked her to a side entrance?"

"Right. You might be in the clear. I guess it all depends on why exactly they're questioning Amador. It might not even be related to him sneaking you into the palace at all. But what else could it be?"

"Who knows, Kori? Everyone in that building is paranoid. It comes from the top and works its way down. Either way, we need to help him, Kori. Loyal staff members with way more responsibility and seniority than Amador, a mid-level officer of the national police, have been executed without cause."

"I know, Anya. Poor Amador. Poor Lidia! But how can we help him?"

"I do not know, Kori, but we need to help him for his sake and for the sake of the mission. What if he talks? What if they torture him?"

"Right. Well, the very first thing is, we probably ought to notify Lidia. She has a right to know. Plus, she may even have some ideas as to what to do. I'm sure she knows other police officers. Maybe someone that she knows on the inside can give us a clearer picture as to why Amador is being held. Or what they might do to him or where they might take him."

"Yes, Lidia can help. But we can't leave the receiver here, Kori."

"No, we can't. Well, listen, why don't you stay here and monitor the conversations taking place in the president's office? I'll ride up to see Lidia and see if we can work on the problem from her end."

"Is the receiver working?"

"I was trying to find the right frequency when you came in. Here, let me try to tune it in." Kori slowly turned a dial on the receiver, hearing static at most points and local FM radio broadcasts at others. Finally, the agents heard the unmistakable sound of Presidente Alonso Estrada.

"Tovar!" he was bellowing. "Come in here. We need to discuss the state dinner next Saturday with the Bolivian ambassador. This menu is unacceptable!"

"There's your man, Anya."

"He is not my man. I am afraid he is going to be disappointed when I do not show up this evening."

"Indeed, you little heartbreaker. Well, I'm sure he'll get over it. In the meantime, the sound is clear as a bell. Nice work with the bugs. You'll probably have to listen to a lot of meaningless crap, but I'm expecting CIA agent Oscar Rentería to report in at any time."

"'Any time' meaning . . . ?"

"Sometime between now and a week from now," Kori grinned.

"Lovely."

"Don't worry. When I get back, we'll start taking shifts. And truthfully, it shouldn't be a week. Let's hope not, anyway. Cooper tells me the batteries in those devices will give us no more than forty-eight hours of uninterrupted service."

"Why no longer?"

"Something about the power that it takes to transmit a radio signal beyond the walls of the palace over any decent amount of distance. But I know that Rentería is due back in the city at any time for more of his so-called reconnaissance. He told Prieto he'd be coming back in a few days and that was two days ago. So it should be soon. Hopefully, we won't have to sit here too long. In the meantime, here, take this energy bar."

"Thanks."

"Now, the other thing we have to hope is that any conversation that takes place with Rentería takes place in that office. It's a big palace, after all."

"It will be in the office," Anya said confidently. "He called it the most important office in the whole of Miranda."

"Yes, I agree with you. Those big stuffed chairs, the comically big desk, the special red phone that goes directly to the palace kitchen . . . he feels strong in that office. It gives him a sense of security." Kori rose and started making for the back door. "I'll text you when I get to the Amador house. And on my way back, I'll pick up something to eat."

"And something to drink?"

"Sure. What do you have in mind?"

"A bottle of vodka might be nice."

Kori chuckled. "I'll see what I can do."

Lidia had heard the news even before Kori arrived. Kori found her sitting on her sofa, wringing her hands, crying intermittently, and softly repeating prayers.

"A friend, the wife of a fellow officer, called," she explained as Kori sat down beside her. "Somebody had seen Pablo taking the ID and lanyard from the security cabinet in the station. These are the days we live in, Señorita Briggs. Rather than approach him, this person waited until he left and then reported him. Officers are turning on each other, you see. Suspicion and mistrust are running rampant. To deflect any unwarranted suspicion from yourself, you turn in somebody else. You prove your loyalty to Estrada's administration by betraying your loyalty to your fellow colleagues. It is madness."

"Did your friend's husband say anything else? Anything about Agent Kovalev?"

"No. All anybody seems to know about is the ID."

"So where is Pablo now?"

"They have transferred him from the palace to the city jail. Oh, it is a terrible jail, señorita. The conditions are deplorable."

"Do you have any idea what Pablo said about taking the ID?"

"No. My husband is strong, Señorita Briggs. No matter what, he will not divulge anything."

"I'm sure."

"Yes, but you see, that only makes it more likely that they will hurt him, to try to make him talk." Lidia began crying all over again.

Kori put her arm around her. "It'll be all right, Lidia. Everything will be all right," she said, although, truthfully, she had no legitimate reason to believe so. "When will you be hearing from your friend again?"

"Her husband is working the night shift. He has promised to check in on Pablo and let us know what is happening, but he might not know anything before the morning. I am scared. Will you stay with me tonight, Señorita Briggs?"

"Of course I will."

"Gracias."

"But listen, Lidia, has anyone from the national police stopped in to see you since they took Pablo?"

"No. Nobody."

"I expect they will. We need to be prepared for the idea that they'll come by here to see if you know anything. You'll be questioned, too."

"Oh, Señorita Kori, you are right! What should we do?"

"Well, the first thing is, I need to hide my moped. I'll take it into the woods behind the house. Nobody can know I'm here."

"Then perhaps you should go," said Lidia. "I do not want to be responsible for anything that might happen to you."

"Don't worry about me; I'll be fine. You shouldn't be alone tonight. Let me hide the moped and I'll come back and fix us some dinner. You need to eat and keep your strength. Frankly, so do I. We'll keep the blinds closed and if anybody knocks on the door, I'll make myself scarce. You got a good hiding place?"

"I suppose you could hide under the house. There is a crawlspace that you can access just outside of the back door, off the kitchen. But it is very small and dark under there."

"I've hidden in worse places. On a stakeout, I once hid in a trash can for an entire night. Now, let me text my partner to let her know what's going on, then I'll go ditch the bike."

You're on your own for the vodka, Kori texted Anya. *I'm staying with Lidia for the night. Will have news on Amador by morning.*

Understood, came Anya's reply. *I'll be here, keeping my ears open.*

It was twilight now and Kori rolled the moped twenty yards into the darkening woods, hiding it behind some brush. By the time she returned, Lidia was in the kitchen already making dinner—*pescado frito*, a fried fish dinner that she was going to serve with plantain fritters.

"Lidia, please," said Kori. "I am happy to do this for you. You should sit."

"No, Señorita Kori, it helps me to have something to do."

"Of course. Well, at least let me give you a hand. What can I do?"

"You can open a bottle of wine."

"Done."

"The glasses are on the shelf there."

Kori opened a bottle and poured two glasses, handing one to Lidia. She stood in the kitchen watching her prepare the batter for the fish and the two chatted about trivial things for a while. Then Lidia talked about the state of her country. "Stable times do not last here," she told Kori. "We seem to always be going through turmoil. But I have never known it like this." She asked about the United States. "What must it be like," she asked, "to live somewhere where you can plan a future? To live in a place that is always stable and secure?"

"Well, it's not *always* stable and secure."

"But your system works."

"Our ideals are wonderful. As a people, however, we don't always live up to them."

"I suppose you would be out of a job if everybody lived according to the best ideals," Lidia said, with a trace of a smile.

"I suppose you're right."

"Your work must be interesting. Tell me more about it."

Kori was about to answer when she heard a vehicle approach outside, the sound of tires rolling over the gravel in the home's driveway. She put her finger to her lips, then slipped out the back door. Two short steps led down to the ground and that distance represented the full height of the crawlspace under the house. Kori lay down on her belly and wriggled herself under the house. It was dark outside now, making the musty crawlspace pitch black. She tried not to think about spiders and snakes and whatever else might be sharing the crawlspace with her but ultimately decided that she had to see what was there. There was barely enough vertical space to move her hand down to her pocket to retrieve her phone and bring it up in front of her, but she managed and then clicked on the phone's flashlight, revealing some cobwebs but nothing too scary. *Better than the trash can*, she thought.

Being directly underneath the kitchen, she could soon make out the sound of footsteps above her on the wooden floor and the muffled voices of Lidia and, from what Kori could gather, two males. She listened closely as the male voices became louder, angrier. Then she could hear the word "wine." *The two glasses!* thought Kori. *Damn! They know someone's here.* She didn't wait. She slid back out of the crawlspace, rose to her feet, pulled out her Glock, and prepared to storm back into the house.

<h1 style="text-align:center">18</h1>

Kori backed up against the exterior wall of the house, just beside the kitchen door. She held her gun tightly, ready to spin forward into the kitchen. But then she heard the footsteps moving away, toward the front door, and the voices fading. She peered into the house and, through the kitchen into the living room, she saw Lidia closing the front door. The men had gone and a moment later, Kori could hear the car driving away. She walked back into the house to see a clearly shaken Lidia.

Kori strode into the living room, taking Lidia by the arm and guiding her to the sofa. "It's okay," she said. "They're gone. Tell me what happened. Did they say who they were? What did they want?"

"They were with *Policia Nacional*. High up in the hierarchy. Much, much higher than Pablo. I'd never seen them before. They asked about Pablo. They wanted to know who he's been with lately. If he's been to any secret meetings. They wanted names. I told them I didn't know anything. I said Pablo hasn't been anywhere. He goes to work and comes home. I pleaded with them to tell me where he was and when he would be released. They wouldn't tell me. Then they walked around the house and into the kitchen and they saw the two wine glasses, Señorita Kori. They became angry. They asked who was here with me."

"What did you say?"

"I told them nobody. I told them I poured the second glass for my husband. In his honor. And to bless him and keep him from harm. They believed me."

"Good thinking, Lidia."

"What is burning? The fish!" Lidia rose and flew into the kitchen, Kori following right behind, seeing the smoke rising from the stove. "Oh, Señorita Kori," Lidia cried, pulling the frying pan off the burner, "our dinner is ruined!"

"Nonsense, Lidia. Where I come from, we call that 'blackened.' I'm sure it will be fine. We'll just be eating it Cajun-style, that's all. Serve it up and I'll pour us a little more wine."

The two ate, both laughing despite the circumstances, at the scorched fish. Lidia supplemented it with the plantains and some homemade bread and the meal was not altogether unsatisfactory. After dinner, the two women sat in the living room and talked some more until, eventually, Kori noticed Lidia's eyes becoming heavy. "You should get some sleep," she told her. "You must be tired. Hopefully, we'll hear from your friend by morning, but in the meantime, I think some rest would do you good."

"*Sí*, I think you are right, Señorita Kori. Will you be okay out here on the sofa?"

"I'll be just fine."

"Then I will say *buenas noches*."

"*Buenas noches*."

Lidia stood and headed toward the bedroom, then stopped and turned.

"Thank you so much for staying with me, Señorita Kori."

"You are more than welcome, Lidia. Everything's going to work out, I'm sure of it."

"Gracias. I believe you."

Lidia went into the bedroom. Kori turned off the lamp in the living room and stretched out on the sofa, underestimating how tired she was. She quickly fell into a deep sleep and was still in its throes four hours later when another car pulled into the driveway. This one she didn't hear. But she heard the jiggle of the front doorknob. Coming out of her slumber, she sat up and instinctively reached for her gun, pointing it at the door, then lowering it as soon as the door opened and Pablo Amador entered the house.

"Señor Amador!" Kori said. "Lidia! Your husband is home!"

Lidia came stumbling out of the bedroom, throwing herself around Amador, who winced in pain.

"Careful, *mi querida*," he said. "My ribs."

"What did they do to you?" Lidia said. "Here, sit down, my husband."

Amador sat on the sofa. By then, Kori had turned on the lamp and could see the damage wrought by Amador's captors. One eye was almost completely swollen shut. His top lip was swollen. There was dried blood under his nose and blood stains on his shirt. His cheeks were dark and puffy. Lidia could see it all too. She crossed herself and sat next to her husband and began to sob.

"There, there," Amador said. "I am okay. I am sure I look worse than I feel. I have had much worse than this in my lifetime. This is nothing."

Kori ran into the kitchen and hurried back with a wet towel. Lidia took it from her and began cleaning her husband's face.

"Señor Amador, what happened?" asked Kori.

"They grabbed me in the palace. Maybe twenty minutes after I let Señorita Kovalev in. But nothing was said about that. Nobody noticed. Instead, they grilled me on the stolen ID. Evidently, someone saw me taking it, although I have no idea who. What is that smell? Was there a fire in here tonight?"

Kori and Lidia both couldn't help but laugh. "I made blackened fish," Lidia said. "Cajun style."

"Señor Amador," Kori said, "your nose might well be broken, but at least your sense of smell is intact."

"Yes, I suppose it is."

"Well, what did you tell the men who interrogated you?"

"I had no legitimate reason to take an identification badge so I just denied it. The record-keeping at the station is very shoddy. There was no way to prove the housekeeper's ID was even in there. They had nothing on me."

"It doesn't look like that kept them from trying to get a confession."

"No, it did not. They took me to the jail and that is when they became more . . . rigorous with their questioning, let us say. But I just kept repeating that I never took any ID badge."

"You see?" said Lidia, turning to Kori. "I knew he would not talk."

"Finally, some other officers, friends of mine, came by and everybody talked it over and it was decided that I could go. One of my friends drove me home."

"Señor Amador, I am so sorry," said Kori. "We never wanted to see you get hurt."

"It is okay, Señorita Briggs. I knew the risk. If anything, I am even more determined now. You can see the state of affairs now, yes? I am a member of the national police and even I had no rights. I had friends at the jail. You can imagine what would happen to a regular citizen with no connections. We are living in a police state and I am ashamed to be a part of it. I am glad I was of help to you. I hope Señorita Kovalev had some success."

"She did. Thanks to you. The bugs are in place and Anya is listening even now to whatever activity is going on in Estrada's office. Probably nothing in the middle of the night, but one never knows. In fact, I should be riding back. I promised Anya we would listen in shifts and I am overdue." Kori stood to leave.

"Thank you for staying with my wife, Kori," said Amador.

"Yes, gracias," said Lidia. "Your kindness will never be forgotten."

"You are more than welcome."

"Kori," said Amador, "what will you do next? When we first talked, you said you were gathering intel. It seems to me as if you already have plenty. And I have a feeling you will get more than you need with your listening devices. Certainly, you have formed an opinion about the problems our nation faces. But what happens now? We will get help from your government, yes? Surely, they cannot stay uninvolved in the tragedy that is playing out here."

"If I am to be honest, Señor Amador, I don't know. That's a decision that comes from high above me. Intervention in another country's politics is a serious matter. But I will tell you that I believe Estrada is a danger not only to your citizens but to the whole region, perhaps to all of South America. Instability in such a large part of the world would have definite repercussions for the United States. Personally, I believe it is within our interests to intervene for the cause of Prieto and the rebels. I will share that opinion with my superior. As it happens, our government may be already leaning that way, as I had mentioned to you. Without going into details, I can tell you that I have seen evidence of the CIA providing aid to *El Principio*. On the other hand, I have also seen indications of the US backing Estrada. It is complicated, like all politics, I suppose. I'm sorry; I wish I had something more definitive to offer you."

"But you told me when we met that you had the ear of your president."

"That is correct."

"You can talk to him, Kori. You can make him understand."

"Again, I will try, Señor Amador. But I am in no position to make any promises. I wish I could."

"I understand, Kori. But do what you can. And please keep yourself safe."

"Gracias, Señor Amador. And you as well."

The dawn was breaking as Kori walked in through the back door of the store. Anya hadn't moved from her position by the receiver.

"Help has arrived, my friend," said Kori. "Get yourself some sleep. It's my shift."

"No need, Kori," said Anya, rising from her chair. "I believe we have everything we need. At least for now."

"No way! Really?"

"Really."

"Do tell."

"Ah, but not until I am fed. Your energy bar was sadly insufficient."

"I understand. Well, the hotel restaurant ought to be open by now. Grab the receiver. Breakfast is on me."

Twenty minutes later—over scrambled eggs, strong coffee, and cornbread muffins called arepas—Anya was relating to Kori what she'd discovered.

"It was after midnight. Truth be told, I was lightly sleeping. It did not occur to me that anybody would be in the presidential office at that hour. I assumed even the guards would be gone. But of course the bugs are voice-activated. When someone begins to talk, they begin to transmit, usually with a short burst of static over the receiver. That is what woke me."

"Was it Estrada?"

"Yes, but then came another voice. I did not recognize it. But then Estrada started calling the other man 'Oscar.'"

"Rentería!"

"Yes. CIA agent Oscar Rentería."

"Bingo! I thought we might be waiting forever for them to meet. Okay, so what did they talk about?"

"Well, Estrada poured Rentería a drink," Anya said, pulling out her scribbled notes.

And then she recounted the conversation:

"What news from the hills?" Estrada asked.

"Things are getting serious," Rentería replied. "The rebels are growing, both in numbers and in resolve."

"I am not concerned."

"It is time to become so, Señor Presidente."

"Then where are the weapons you have promised?"

"They are on their way."

"That is what you said last time, Oscar."

"We hit a snag. But it is simply a matter of paperwork, I assure you. The weapons are, as we speak, sitting in a warehouse in the marine terminal in the Port of Baltimore. The proper documentation is now being arranged. You must understand the difficulty of this. The necessity of secrecy, the forging of signatures, and all the other hurdles that must be overcome. The sale of the weapons is not something that has been approved by our president."

"But you are the CIA, Oscar. You have told me that you can circumvent the president anytime you want. You have boasted of this, in fact. You have told me that such a mission is easy for you."

"Well, yes, relatively speaking. But that doesn't mean that something of this magnitude can happen overnight. It will happen soon, though. Perhaps this week. Then, the weapons will be shipped to Miami, and then here."

"This is too much time. You must make it happen sooner."

"I will do what I can. In the meantime, might I suggest another course of action? Perhaps a course of action that might represent a more . . . permanent solution to your problem?"

"What course of action would that be?"

"An idea I have been toying with for a little while now. It is what I wanted to talk to you about tonight."

"I am listening."

"*El Principio* is like a snake, Señor Presidente. A snake can be dangerous if it is poisonous and you do not see it. But if you can see it, you can kill it and it will be dangerous no more. And everybody knows that to kill a snake, you have to cut off its head. We can see this snake, Señor Presidente. We know where it lives. Let us cut off its head and then we can be done with it once and for all."

"Prieto?"

"Prieto. The guerrilla band will disintegrate. There is no one to take his place and the movement will collapse without him. But it must happen soon before the rebels grow more brave. Before they can enlist more of the citizenry to their side. Before it will be too late."

"Who will kill him, Oscar? You?"

"No, no, no. His rebels would kill me in turn."

"But how can we get an assassin into his camp?"

"That is the beauty of the plan. We won't need to, you see. Prieto will come to us."

"Oh? How so?"

"I happen to know that Prieto will be returning to the city. In three days, in fact. He will be meeting secretly with several underground groups. He wants to come out of the hills and get closer to the people, to rally them, to motivate them. He is looking to grow the rebel cause past a point from which revolution will be a foregone conclusion."

"He cannot do so. The people love their presidente."

"Well, yes, of course. Of course. Nevertheless, we should not take chances, Señor Presidente. I know where Prieto will be on Thursday night. He will be attending a meeting in the basement of the Cathedral of the Holy Savior. It would be an easy thing to post a sharpshooter across the plaza on the roof of the National Assembly building. Naturally, Prieto will not want to leave the building through the front doors, but there is a side door that opens into the plaza. I will convince him that the rear doors are unsafe and that he'd be better off exiting into the plaza from the side door because nobody from the government would dare hurt him in such an open place. He will have guerrilla soldiers with him, of course, but no one would guess that a sharpshooter would be positioned across the plaza. It will be the perfect opportunity. A single shot and this rebel band will no longer be a thorn in your side."

Estrada was quiet for a moment, turning the idea over in his mind. "But it might not go over with those who are in sympathy with the rebels. We must be careful, Oscar. How do we know the plan will not backfire? How do we know that the assassination of the guerrilla leader will not result in more people leaning toward the terrible cause of the rebels? We must not make a martyr out of that disgusting traitor."

"Simple, Señor Presidente. You will take no responsibility for the killing. In fact, you will blame the killing on a dissenting group of rebels, a faction that is in active competition with Prieto's group."

"Who?"

"Does it matter? You control the media. You can get any story out to the people that you wish. Look at what you've managed to do with the supposed nuclear program. Everyone believes you have nuclear weapons ready to launch."

Estrada chuckled. "Yes, indeed. We've sold that well, have we not? But of course, I have you to thank for getting Prieto to believe we are manufacturing sarin gas."

"Yes, he bought that easily. Just as the population will buy the story we will manufacture about the assassin. The news outlets will report that a band of guerrillas even more evil than Prieto's band has killed Prieto. No more needs to be said. We will whisk your shooter from the sight and then parade some random prisoner in front of the people and claim that he was the assassin. Someone nobody knows, of course. An anonymous thief will do. You will show that the law prevails, even if an act of violence has been carried out against an enemy of yours. The prisoner will be summarily executed. You will look like a hero even to the remaining rebels."

"And the remaining rebels will disperse," Estrada said excitedly. "The rebel movement will die!"

"*Sí*, Señor Presidente. The rebel movement will die because you will have cut off its head. Like the vile snake that it is."

"Brilliant, Oscar."

Anya heard laughter at that point and the clinking of glasses. Presidente Alonso Estrada was clearly well pleased.

19

— • —

Kori ordered more coffee from the hotel restaurant's waitress and leaned back in her seat, her brow furrowed. "So what is Rentería's game?" she said. "Why is he simultaneously helping Prieto while plotting to kill him? Those weren't pop guns I saw at the camp. And I don't believe that story he conjured up about the paperwork delay. That's total BS. Those weapons shipped. But they didn't ship to Estrada. They shipped to his enemies."

"It's puzzling," Anya agreed. "He seems to be playing both sides against the middle, but for what reason?"

"Right. For what reason? Just what position is the CIA taking, anyway?" Kori pulled out her phone. "The chief has had Cooper and Foster working on this. Maybe they know something."

Eaglethorpe picked up on one ring. "Talk to me, Agent Briggs. What's going on?"

"Well, what's going on, Chief, is that the CIA agent stationed in San Benito is pretty heavily involving himself in this country's affairs."

"What a shock."

"The problem is, he's involving himself equally on both sides. Agent Kovalev just listened to a conversation that took place between Estrada and Rentería and now we have even less of an idea as to what side the CIA is on than we did before."

"Maybe we can help, Kori. Cooper and Foster have done some digital sleuthing. I don't know how they did it, nor am I even going to ask. Hell, I probably wouldn't understand it anyway. But this morning, they uncovered a shipping manifest of weapons destined for the main base of the Mirandan Armed Forces, right there in San Benito."

"Really? When are the weapons shipping?"

"They shipped two weeks ago. They should be there by now."

"What kind of weapons, Chief?"

"Well, let's see . . . I have the manifest right here. Thirty M14 rifles, twenty-five M240 machine guns, fifty M500 shotguns, twenty sniper rifles, twenty grenade launchers—"

"Chief, don't you see? That's the shipment I saw at the rebel camp. All boxed up like Christmas presents. I mean, I can't swear to the numbers, but it seems pretty coincidental that there would be another shipment so close in description to that one. It's got to be the same shipment. The weapons made it to Miranda all right, but they never made it to Estrada's military base. For some reason, they were rerouted."

"Hang on, let me get Cooper and Foster on the line."

"How's it going, Kori?" came Cooper's voice, echoed moments later by Foster's.

"It's going okay, guys. We're just a little befuddled."

"Listen, gentlemen," said Eaglethorpe, "Agent Briggs tells me your shipping manifest most likely represents the same cache of weapons she discovered at the rebel camp. Could it be that you have the destination wrong?"

"No way, Chief," said Cooper. "That manifest came with a memorandum that was very specific about where they were to be shipped. There could be no mistake. We found both the manifest and the accompanying memorandum in an encrypted file-sharing site that only a few CIA operatives can access. And us, of course. I can't take credit. Foster was the one who hacked it."

"All in a day's work," said Foster.

"So, as far as we know," said Eaglethorpe, "the CIA believes the weapons went to Estrada's army. Correct?"

"We've seen nothing that contradicts that," said Cooper. "Needless to say, we're monitoring that site regularly. We figure it'll take a few days before anybody there notices our fingerprints. We're bouncing through a slew of secure servers all over the globe, so it won't do them any good, but eventually they'll wise up and shut the site down and reopen it elsewhere."

"But if the CIA believes the weapons shipped to the army base," Kori asked, "then who's Rentería getting his orders from? I mean, somebody directed the diversion of the shipment. Maybe someone higher up than what you guys uncovered? Maybe there's an even more exclusive file-sharing site somewhere."

"That wouldn't make sense," said Eaglethorpe, "because everything we've seen seems to indicate that Secretary of

State Lloyd Higgins is, in fact, directing the CIA to help Estrada."

"Really?"

"Yes. And it doesn't get any higher than that. That's the other thing we uncovered. Tell her, Agent Foster."

"It's true, Kori. We've identified at least three different occasions where Higgins met with Cedric Doyle of Worldwide Petroleum and Chemical, the major importer of Estrada's oil. Lowkey meetings, too. Nothing public. Within a week of each meeting, Higgins's bank account balance took a nice bump. Not his personal account, of course. Turns out we managed to find an offshore account that belongs to the secretary."

"So he *is* being bribed," said Kori.

"It would appear so. We've also uncovered phone records of Higgins speaking directly to Estrada. Doyle talks to him all the time, too. The secretary of state is definitely calling the shots and he's being well-compensated for supporting Estrada's regime. The memorandum directing the shipping of the weapons references Higgins himself."

"Really?" said Kori. "By name?"

"No, and that's what threw us at first. Someone code-named 'The Wanderer' was behind the orders, but for the longest time, we couldn't connect the name to Higgins."

"So how did you?"

Cooper chuckled. "Like all good espionage: accidentally. We happened to be following him around a couple of days ago. He drove to Capitol Cove Marina and that's where it all came together."

"How?"

"*The Wanderer* is the name of his boat."

"Nice work," said Kori. "Accidental or not."

"Thanks. Anyway, we should tell you that the memorandum mentions additional shipments. What you saw is not the end of it. We believe at least three more shipments of weapons are headed to Miranda."

"Cripes," said Kori, "that's going to be a lot of firepower. If it all ends up with *El Principio*, they'll be a viable revolutionary force."

"Agent Briggs," said Eaglethorpe, "we need to determine why that first shipment was directed to *El Principio*'s camp when the secretary of state is pulling the CIA's strings to support Estrada. Is it possible it was somehow hijacked by the rebels themselves?"

"Well if it was, it was done with the full knowledge of CIA agent Oscar Rentería. He knows it's in the rebel camp. That's why he was so suspicious of my wandering around the camp that night. Plus, Anya overheard him making really lame excuses as to why the shipment hasn't yet shown up at the Mirandan military base."

"So it was Rentería himself who redirected the shipment," said Eaglethorpe.

"It must have been."

"So he's helping the rebels, contravening his orders from Secretary of State Higgins."

"No, Chief, that doesn't make sense either. Get this: the other thing Anya overheard was that Rentería has hatched a plan to assassinate rebel leader Lucas Prieto."

"Assassinate Prieto? Are you sure?"

"Yep. He's got it all figured out and Estrada's fully on board."

"So why would Rentería arrange for the rerouting of weapons to help the rebels while at the same time arranging for the assassination of their leader?"

"It's as if he's working on his own," Foster chimed in. "Like he's got his own agenda. But what?"

"I'll tell you what!" Kori said, the scope of Rentería's actions suddenly coming together in her mind. "Oh, man, I can't believe I hadn't thought of it earlier. His is the oldest agenda in the book. I know what he's after, guys!"

"And what's that?" Eaglethorpe asked.

"Power."

"Power?"

"Chief, Oscar Rentería has done such an effective job of infiltrating the guerrilla camp that he's earned Prieto's unconditional trust. He came to Prieto about six months ago calling himself Fernando Vallejo with a concocted story that he had worked with the ministry of internal affairs. He claimed to know all the government's secrets. And of course, because of his CIA relationship with Estrada, he actually does. He had instant credibility. And Prieto's become positively enamored with him. He called him his right-hand man and *compadre*. More importantly, he called him his second-in-command. I'm sure that once the weapons showed up, courtesy of 'Fernando Vallejo,' his position was cemented."

"Meaning what exactly, Agent Briggs?"

"Meaning that once he has Estrada assassinate Prieto, Rentería will move from second-in-command to first.

Don't you get it? Rentería is retiring from the CIA and he's planning on one hell of a retirement party. He's going to lead a revolution. Fernando Vallejo is poised to become the new leader of the Republic of Miranda."

20

"We have to stop him," Kori continued. "We have to alert the CIA that their man in Miranda has gone rogue."

"Easier said than done," Eaglethorpe said. "Think about it, Briggs. What's our evidence? A bugged conversation and the discovery of a secret cache of weapons by under-cover infiltration. How do we present either of those to the CIA without giving ourselves away? We mustn't compromise our secrecy. We've worked too hard to maintain it."

"I see what you're saying, Chief."

"No, we have to handle this ourselves. Our only move, Kori, is for you to find a way to warn Prieto about the impending assassination attempt. You have to stop it."

"Understood."

"But, wait a moment," said Cooper, "are you sure that's what we do? Chief, so far, Agents Briggs and Kovalev have been doing surveillance. And, I might add, doing it very well."

"Thanks, Coop," said Kori.

"But as soon as we warn Prieto," Cooper continued, "it seems to me that we cross a line. At that point, we involve ourselves. We put ourselves in the middle of things. Isn't that beyond the scope of the mission? Isn't that beyond the scope of Rampart? Mind you, I'm not saying it's not the right move; I'm just asking the question."

"And you are right to do so, Agent Cooper," said Eaglethorpe. "We involve ourselves in the affairs of other countries only carefully and judiciously and, typically, only when the interests of the United States are at stake. Or—and I think this is the pertinent detail in this case—when an American has already involved him or herself. Rentería is a US citizen. The United States is therefore already involved in Miranda, vis-à-vis CIA agent Oscar Rentería. And that means the US is responsible for his actions."

"Not necessarily," Cooper countered. "As a rogue, he's not operating as an agent of the United States. He's on his own. In fact, he's apparently forfeiting his US citizenship in favor of a new identity. He's no more an American than Alonso Estrada is. 'Fernando Vallejo' is a Mirandan."

"Doesn't matter," said Eaglethorpe. "We know better. We know that the only reason he's gotten to the position where he is, one bullet away from leading the rebels to war against the Mirandan regime, is because of his employment by a US intelligence agency. That makes us responsible for him. I don't mean Rampart specifically, but the fact is, we're the only ones who know what's about to go down. We have a duty to step in. Especially, in case anybody has forgotten, when nuclear weapons are potentially in the picture."

"Yes, well, Chief, that's another thing," Kori said. "As it turns out, we discovered something else. The nuclear weapons program is as big a fake ploy as the sarin gas ruse."

"Really?"

"Really."

"Well, that's what I'm talking about," said Cooper. "That gives us even less of a reason to jump in. Without WMDs, what's our justification for being there?"

"Kori, what do you think?" Foster asked.

"I say we stop Rentería on general principle," Kori replied. "We have to stop him because it's the right thing to do. Look, guys, I appreciate a philosophical discussion as much as the next person, but this Rentería guy is bad news. Period. And you know who's worse? Presidente Alonso Estrada. I think this goes beyond the question of who's a citizen of what country, and who should be involved and who should not be involved. Don't you see? We have to step in as human beings. We have to not only stop Rentería, but we also have to help Prieto give the Mirandans their freedom from the brutal and repressive regime of Estrada."

"Whoa, one step at a time," said Eaglethorpe. "I respect your passion, Briggs, but that's going too far at this point. That *would* be crossing a line. We're not in the business of overthrowing governments, even if, as you say, it's the right or 'human' thing to do. Once we make that a precedent, where does it stop? Now, look, the proper play at this point is to find a way to warn Prieto and to continue to surveil Rentería. And then we'll reexamine things as we go. That's fair, isn't it?" Everyone voiced their general agreement and Eaglethorpe closed the conversation with, "Get to it, Agent Briggs. And keep me informed."

Kori hung up, took a swig of her coffee, and looked across the table at Anya. "You know, I saw you shaking your head, my friend, as I was making my argument for helping the rebels. Are you still not convinced that Estrada's regime is an evil force that needs to be deposed?"

"Oh, I am very much convinced, my friend," Anya replied. "I'm just not convinced that intervening is the right thing to do."

"Hmm. Well, as it happens, the chief agrees with you. He does believe, however, that we have to find a way to warn Prieto. The problem is, I have no idea how to find him. Even if I knew where I was the night I stumbled upon the camp, I'm sure they're in a different place by now; they were planning on moving the next day. God only knows where in the hills they are."

"How about the bartender? Maybe he can help us again."

"I don't know how many times I can go back to that well," Kori said, "but I'm not seeing much of a choice. The bar doesn't open until noonish. We probably both ought to catch some z's in the meantime. I didn't sleep too well on the Amador's sofa and you've been up all night listening to the receiver. Why don't we meet in the bar around, say, one? Here, I'll get the check."

"Thanks."

"Hey, no problem," Kori smiled. "We brunettes have to stick together."

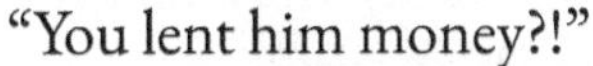

"You lent him money?!"

Kori had gotten a little nap and decided to call her mother before heading down to the bar to meet Anya. Now she wished she hadn't.

"Well, of course, dear," Joan Briggs replied. "The situation with his sister has become dire. Kori, if she doesn't get that kidney transplant, she'll die. I mean, what was I supposed to do? I can't let that happen. Oh, of course Bertram declined my offer at first. He's a proud man, Kori."

"I'm sure."

"But then he started to cry. Oh, Kori, it was so sad to see Bertram like that. And so I insisted. Finally, he agreed and we went to the bank and I got him a cashier's check."

"A cashier's check, Mom?"

"Yes, his sister is in California, remember? I couldn't very well give him a personal check, Kori. It would take too long to clear. He needs the money now. In fact, he's on his way to Sacramento even as we speak."

"Mom . . . " Kori hesitated, afraid to finish the question, "how much exactly did you give Bertram?"

"Thirty thousand dollars."

"Thirty thousand dollars?!"

"Well, yes, that's what he needed. It's a kidney transplant, Kori, not a pedicure. But, listen, here's the good news. Bertram said that by next week, he'll have full access to his cash. He's been talking with his attorneys and everything is being worked out. He's going to pay me right back. 'With interest,' he told me. Of course, I wouldn't dream of charging him interest."

"Mom, listen, how much do you really know about this guy? I mean, have you ever been to his house? Ever met any friends of his or anything?"

"No. But, Kori, I know everything I need to know about him. Bertram is a wonderful man. I can't wait for you to meet him."

"I can't wait either. What did you say his last name was?"

"Summers."

"And you made the check out to his name?"

"Of course. Oh, Kori, you'll like him, I'm sure. As soon as he gets back, the three of us will have to get together for dinner."

"Sure, Mom. That would be good. Dinner with Bertram sounds terrific. Say, do you happen to have a picture of him you can text me?"

"Oh, yes, we had the waiter take a picture of us at lunch the other day. You'll see how handsome he is."

"Great, Mom." Then Kori was silent, not at all sure what to say. Her mother was quite taken with Bertram, that was clear. It was also clear that she'd been taken *by* Bertram. But what if his story checked out? Kori didn't want to throw cold water on the first serious relationship her mother had had in years. And even in the worst case, which also seemed to be the most probable case, she didn't want to see her mother get hurt. Kori was sure that with the resources of Rampart, she could get Joan's money back. But if Joan

came to realize she'd been had, and that Bertram's atten-
tions had been nothing more than part of a scam, it would
break her heart. That would be even worse than the loss of
the money.

"What's the matter, dear?" Joan said. "You're not saying
anything."

"Oh, uh . . . nothing, Mom. Just do me a favor and keep
me posted on Bertram's sister, would you?"

"Of course I will. He promised to give me updates. He
just phoned me from the airport before you called to say
his flight is on schedule."

"That's great, Mom. Well, listen, I better be going."
Then she forced a cheerful tone and said, "We'll talk soon,
okay? And don't forget that picture."

Kori hung up and immediately called Darren Cooper
back at Rampart HQ.

"Kori, what's up? Don't tell me you've gotten to Prieto
already."

"No, we're still working on that, Coop. But listen, I need
a favor."

"Shoot."

"I need you to hack into my mother's cell phone
records."

"Really? Your mother's?"

"Yes. She just took a call from someone named Bertram
Summers. I'm guessing that's not his real name. Track the
number down, would you?"

"Sure. So what's the scoop?"

"The scoop is I think this guy just took my mom for
thirty grand."

"Wow, no kidding?"

"No kidding. Evidently, he's working some con where he's preying on lonely, older women. He's convinced my mom that his sister needs a kidney transplant. He's wealthy, of course, but—wouldn't you know it?—he's not very liquid right now."

"Oh, boy. Let me guess. He's going to pay her right back."

"Within a week."

"Damn. Thirty grand is a lot. Sorry to hear that, Kori."

"Thanks. The worst part is that I think my mom was really falling for this guy."

"Ouch."

"We need to get the money back, Coop. But, listen, whatever his real name is, he's apparently set up a bank account somewhere in the name of Bertram Summers. My mom wrote a cashier's check to that name."

"So he's a pro."

"Right. He's most likely created a complete identity for himself. My guess is he'll deposit the money, withdraw it in cash, then scram. Probably he'll find another lonely, older woman to con. I'm sure my mom's not the first, and unless we find this chucklehead, she won't be the last. Anyway, I've got a picture of him that my mom just texted me. I'll forward it along."

"Piece of cake, Kori. I'll scour the database for the cell number and the alias and we'll run a facial recognition search. He's as good as caught. Give me a couple of hours, okay?"

"Thank, Coop. You're the best."

At one, nobody was in the bar except for Kori and Anya and, of course, the ever-present Santiago. The agents ordered drafts and Kori requested, once again, access to the rebels. She had some follow-up questions that her editor at the *Post* was insisting she ask Lucas Prieto. "I really hate to bother you with this, but could you please arrange it again?" she said.

"It did not turn out very well last time," Santiago said. "I heard about the truck being stopped. I heard about the killings."

"Yes, I know," said Kori. "And believe me, it's not our intent to get anyone hurt or killed. The fact is, the truck would have been stopped regardless. Nobody knew I was in the back. The truck was making a return to the camp with supplies that it would have made anyway."

"True."

"So will you help us?"

Santiago thought for a moment. "I will leave it up to others," he said finally. "I will pass along your request. That is all that I can do. I cannot imagine it will be granted. What is to be gained by it, after all? Another interview. More questions. Do you not have enough to write your article?"

Kori glanced at Anya and then leaned in toward Santiago. "Pass along that I might have more than questions.

We've been doing some digging and we have some information that, believe me, is in the best interests of the rebels to know. Comandante Prieto will be grateful, I assure you."

"What information? From where?"

Kori contemplated telling Santiago of the assassination plot. But why would he believe her? How would she know of the plot without somehow having inside information from the palace? And that would mean to Santiago that she was connected with the regime in some way. And she couldn't tell him her discovery came by way of a listening device. That would compromise her cover as a journalist.

"I can't say," said Kori at last. "But you have to trust me, Santiago. Believe me, I have seen enough of Estrada's dictatorial rule. Although as a journalist I am supposed to be unbiased, I find that my sympathies are with Prieto."

Anya nodded. "It is true, señor. We are both having difficulties remaining neutral."

"You must remember," Kori continued, "I was almost killed myself in that truck stop. It was luck that I am here today. And I would not risk such a trip again unless I knew it was important. Will you trust me, Santiago?"

Santiago sensed sincerity in Kori's voice. "Ah, it is just as well that you do not tell me," he said. "I should probably not know. I know too much as it is. Okay, señorita. I will trust you. I will mention that you have information. Come back this evening."

With a few hours of downtime, the agents decided to spend the afternoon scoping out the Cathedral of the Holy Savior, the planned site of the assassination. It was in the main plaza of the city, the same plaza where stood the fifty-foot-high bronze statue of Presidente Alonso Estrada. He was standing with his arm raised, palm up as if beckoning to his people. The generous, benevolent, wise leader. People walked by, but Kori noticed that few seemed to take any interest in the huge sculpture. Nobody, for instance, was posing in front of it for pictures.

The cathedral was on one side of the plaza, and on the other side, kitty-corner to it, was the National Assembly building, a large five-story neoclassical structure where the legislative body of Miranda supposedly met to make laws and shape the direction of the country, a body theoretically made up of democratically elected officials. In truth, the assembly still met but decided nothing. Estrada used it for show. If any legislation took place in the National Assembly building, it took place in accordance with Estrada's wishes and the result was arrived at always by Estrada's command, either by bribe or by threat. Nevertheless, he made a big show of how all his edicts and directives were arrived at by the popular vote of the "legislature of the people," as he called it.

"Kori," said Anya, pointing to the Assembly building, "from that corner of the roof, one would have a clear shot at the cathedral."

"Right," said Kori. "It's a flat roof, too, with a balustrade running around it. Someone could just lie flat up there; no one would see a sniper with a high-powered rifle."

Anya looked across the plaza to the cathedral. "There's the side door Rentería spoke of. A straight shot from the Assembly building. A hundred yards, I would say, maybe less."

"C'mon, Anya. Let's check out the cathedral."

They strolled across the plaza and climbed the many steps leading to the front entrance of the grand, historical, Spanish-colonial-style cathedral. They walked in through the tall, heavy doors, and on into the narthex. The dozen or so people inside the church were a mix of worshippers lighting candles at a long table in front of the altar cross, and tourists taking cell phone pictures of the beautiful nave and the high, arched ceiling.

"Gorgeous," Kori said in a hushed voice.

"Indeed," Anya agreed.

"Look, there's the side door."

They walked around the edge of the nave to the side door, about three-quarters of the way toward the altar. Kori nudged the door open an inch or two and looked across the plaza toward the Assembly building.

"Yep, it's a straight shot, all right," she said. "If he so much as sticks his head out of this door, he'll be a dead duck." She closed the door. "C'mon, let's go. It looks like afternoon mass might be starting soon."

As the two agents began walking back toward the main doors, Anya stopped and grabbed Kori by the elbow. "Wait here," she said. Kori watched as Anya walked up to the front of the cathedral, to the altar. She reached for a votive candle from the table, took a match, and lit it. She sat the candle down and made her way back to Kori and the two went out through the doors and back down the stairs to the street.

"Think it'll help?" Kori asked.

"Couldn't hurt," said Anya. "In a situation like this, one must use every tool at one's disposal."

"Señoritas!" came a voice behind them.

The two-wheeled around to see a smallish woman in dark jeans and a pink V-neck T-shirt bounding after them down the steps. She was young, with a pretty face and sad, round eyes. Anya recognized her from inside the cathedral. She had been in the first pew, her head bowed in prayer.

"You are from the US, aren't you?" she asked.

"Yes," said Kori.

"With the newspaper. Is that right?"

"Um, yes. How did you know?"

"I come downtown from time to time. I live in Barrio Descarado, just on the edge of the city. I come here to pray, and I come here to get news. There has been talk of a beautiful, American reporter. Perhaps two female reporters. You are both dressed too well to live here and I guessed you might be the reporters from the US people are speaking of."

"Good guess. What can we do for you?"

"You have to help us, señoritas."

"What's your name?" Kori asked.

The woman looked furtively around and lowered her voice. "I will tell you my name, but you must not publish it."

"Don't worry. We won't. I can promise you that."

"My name is Luna Segura. My husband's name is Guillermo. We have a son—Pedro. My husband is missing. He was taken by the police in the middle of the night. I pray for him, but I do not believe I will ever see him again. He is a victim of *las purgas*. You must do what you can, señoritas. The world must know. We are dying, you see. All of us. All of Miranda is dying."

21

— · —

Kori, Anya, and Luna Segura sat on a plaza bench near a fountain that no longer spouted water. The agents listened as Luna recounted the harrowing night when the members of *Policia Nacional* stormed into her house and whisked Guillermo away.

"You see, my husband worked in the city for the tourism bureau. He had been approached one day by a coworker. There was a meeting the friend wanted Guillermo to attend in the basement of a church. An opposition group. Guillermo went to the meeting even though I tried to talk him out of it. I feared for his safety. But these groups were popping up all over. Estrada has shut down internet access to all but government-sanctioned sites, but those opposing him are getting the word out anyway. They are leaving stacks of printed leaflets around the city at bus stops and metro stations and in the barrios. The opposition is coming together, of course, under *El Principio*. Estrada is fuming. The purges are more frequent. The cars come around late at night, señoritas. They take husbands and fathers, sometimes whole families. The missing . . . they never come back, you see."

Kori and Anya exchanged glances.

"Well, anyway," Luna continued, "Guillermo went to the meeting. Two nights later came a knock on the door: four officers of *Policia Nacional*. 'We need you to come with us,' one of them said to my husband. 'To answer a few questions. It should not take long.' Oh, señoritas, I knew better. I begged the officers not to take Guillermo."

Luna paused and took a deep breath, trying to compose herself. "I am sorry," she said.

"Please," said Anya, "take your time."

"Gracias, señorita. Well, of course they left with my husband. The whole thing was only a matter of minutes. Pedro slept through it. The next morning, he asked, 'Where is Papá?' I told him he'd be back soon. And I told him that the following day and the day after that. Then I stopped saying it. Now, I fear I do not know what to say."

Kori recognized the story. It was the same one Pablo Amador had recounted, the arrest that made him question everything about the Estrada regime, the arrest that had him asking for beat duty in the streets so he could be away from the inner workings of Estrada's police force—*Estrada's own SS*, Amador had called it. Truthfully, there were probably dozens of similar stories, maybe hundreds. But for reasons she didn't fully understand herself, Kori couldn't shake the idea that Luna's house was the same one Amador had spoken of.

"Señora Segura," she started.

"Please call me Luna."

"Luna, tell me something. Does your son have a poster of *fútbol* star Marco Quezada above his bed?"

"*Sí*," Luna replied, a surprised look on her face. "How do you know that?"

"I can't really say, I'm afraid, but I think you might like to know that at least one member of *Policia Nacional* switched sides that night. Or at least turned away from Estrada. And I believe that others will follow. My opinion, based on what we have been witnessing, is that Estrada is greatly underestimating the level of dissension among the Mirandan people."

"Oh, let us hope so, señorita. Of course it comes too late for my beautiful Guillermo."

"Now don't say that. You mustn't give up hope. He might still be alive and perhaps they will release him soon." Even as Kori said it out loud, she knew it wasn't true.

Luna nodded slightly and said nothing. Kori immediately felt guilty for saying something that to Luna must have so clearly sounded naïve or, worse, condescending.

"And where is your son now?" Anya asked, breaking the silence.

"Pedro is with a neighbor. I do not bring him into the city. I like to come to the cathedral to pray by myself."

"Of course."

"And sometimes I go to the underground meetings. I suppose I am becoming something of a revolutionary. It is my way of continuing Guillermo's interest in seeing our land become free one day. But, señoritas, you must do what you can to expose the true condition of our country. The outside world must know what is happening here.

Perhaps you already know this. But when I saw you, I felt compelled to tell you myself."

"We understand," said Kori. "We'll do what we can."

"And now I fear I have taken too much of your time," said Luna. "Thank you so much for listening to me. You have been very gracious."

"You're more than welcome," said Kori.

"Be safe, señoritas," Luna said, and then she rose and walked away, past the statue of Presidente Alonso Estrada, out of the plaza, and into the forlorn streets of San Benito.

"Well?" Kori asked. "You can't possibly still think we ought to stay out of this country's disgraceful affairs."

Kori and Anya were having dinner and drinks at the same outdoor café where they'd eaten before. It was close to the hotel; it felt safe.

"To be honest, I do not know what I think right now," Anya replied. "Estrada is a murdering thug, there is no doubt. I would love to see him deposed. But what would that take, Kori? Are you in favor of violent revolution? War and bloodshed?"

"Of course not. Prieto doesn't think it would come to that and I think he might be right. Think about it, Anya. With another three shipments of weapons and more re-cruits for his guerrilla army—which is obviously the reason he's attending these secret meetings back here in the capital—he might just make enough noise to where Estrada's generals see the writing on the wall and switch allegiances. They're not stupid. Surely they feel the momentum shifting. You can feel it, right? Revolution is in the air. The city tingles with it. Frankly, it's the only thing that's giving this city any life at all."

"Yes, I feel it. I have felt it since I got here. And you might be right. But one thing is for sure. The picture changes with Lucas Prieto's assassination."

"It sure does. Oscar Rentería is obviously power-mad. He has no sympathy for the people of this country. If he did, he wouldn't be pushing for Prieto's murder. But, Anya, he has done a masterful job of ingratiating himself not just with Prieto, but with the rebel army. I noticed the men in the camp looked up to him. He is sanctioned by nobody less than Prieto himself. He would easily take control of the rebel army. I can't imagine there would even be a discussion. Prieto's men will turn immediately to Rentería. 'Fernando Vallejo.' But something tells me Rentería wouldn't care if the revolution was a bloody one. Whatever gets him the palace."

"He might be counting on a bloody revolution, Kori."

"How so?"

"You have postulated that the generals would switch sides, that they would feel the momentum changing. But with Prieto's death, maybe the momentum does not change. Sure, the guerrilla army might fall into line behind Rentería, but maybe the populace does not."

"Hmm . . . go on."

"What does the populace know about Rentería? He is not the one making speeches and inspiring people. Is he even recognized outside of the rebel camp? Prieto's death might—how do you say?—take the wind out of the sails. If the populace is not behind the rebels, then the generals will most likely stick with Estrada. And if that is the case, the only way Rentería wins himself the presidential palace is through blood."

"You're right, Anya. Then we've got to keep Prieto alive."

"But there is something else, Kori. Assuming we can get a meeting with Prieto, how do we know he will believe our warning? You said he is close to Rentería. *Compadres*, yes?"

"True."

"In his eyes, we are journalists. Who is he more likely to believe? Strangers from the US, or his loyal and trusted *compadre*?"

"Then we've got to convince him we're intelligence agents."

"What if that seems to him like a betrayal?"

"At first, it probably will. I mean, he was counting on a big spread in the *Washington Post*. But once we explain everything, I think he'll be pretty damn grateful we came along."

"Yes, I suppose you are right. Let us hope so."

"Sure, I'm right. Now, what do you say we order two more of these drinks and then get to the hotel bar to see what Santiago has to tell us? What did you call them?"

"They are 'guarapitas.' Rum, grenadine, orange juice, and a few other things."

"Well, they hit the spot. Take out the OJ and the few other things, and maybe even the grenadine, and you'd really have something." Kori waved to the waiter. *"Señor? Dos guarapitas, por favor."*

As the waiter went to fetch the drinks, Kori turned to Anya and said, "Listen, I have to make a quick call to Agent Cooper."

"Of course," said Anya. Kori had told her about the situation her mother had fallen into and Anya listened along as Kori got the latest.

"Bertram Summer," Cooper reported. "Real name: Vincent Helm. The guy's been in and out of prison most of his adult life."

"Damn," said Kori. "I was hoping I was wrong, Coop."

"'Fraid not, Kori. He's a bona fide con artist. He got out of Hazelton Federal Correctional Institution in West Virginia just six months ago. He was serving time for stock fraud. Had a little Ponzi scheme going. Anyway, looks like he settled in Alexandria and I guess that's where he met your mom. Apparently, he wasn't quite rehabilitated."

"Can you find him, Coop?"

"I'm already on it, Kori. You know Ford and Baldwin?"

"The detective agency?"

"Yep. Best and biggest in the city. They owe me a favor. They've got a couple of their best guys on it. I'll bet they'll track him down in twenty-four hours or less."

"Nice. Thanks, Coop. I owe you a beer."

"Don't mention it. So what do you want us to do with him? Have him arrested?"

"No, I don't think so. My mother would have to press charges and testify. Worse, she'd know she was used. I can't stand the thought of that. I've got a better idea."

Kori finished giving Cooper her instructions, she and Anya finished their guarapitas, and then it was back to the hotel. In the bar, Santiago poured two drafts for the agents while saying very little. Other people were in the bar and Santiago was practicing an especially high degree of nonchalance. He poured drinks for other guests and chatted lightly with them. Eventually, he returned to the agents with a bowl of complimentary beer nuts that he delivered with a cocktail napkin. He smiled courteously, said nothing, and then stepped to the other side of the bar.

Kori glanced down at the napkin, then quickly folded it and slipped it into her handbag. She downed what was left of her beer and Anya did the same. Then they rose from their seats, Kori tossed a few Mirandan dollars on the bar, and the agents exited the bar, strode through the hotel lobby, and went out into the street.

Kori pulled out the napkin and unfolded it. "It's an address."

"That's all?"

"Well, and a note that says 'tonight.'"

"Do you recognize the address?" Anya asked.

"No. Let me look it up." Kori pulled out her phone and punched the address into her map app. "West of here. Just outside the city. Looks like a warehouse in another industrial area. An hour's ride, more or less."

"You think Prieto will be there?"

"I don't know. We know that he's starting to come back into San Benito to meet with underground groups. I suppose it could be a meeting."

"Right. Or maybe it's just some guerrillas waiting for us who will take us to the current encampment."

"Sure, that could be it. Well, only one way to find out. Let's grab the bikes. It'll be dark by the time we get there, but at least we'll have daylight for most of the ride."

The agents rode their mopeds along the main highway that left the city to the west, the sun setting in front of them, finally dipping below the horizon and leaving a blackening sky in its wake. They exited in an area that did not look dissimilar to the area where the faux sarin plant was. Same kind of rundown buildings, many with broken or boarded-up windows. The surrounding streets were empty of people. Streetlamps were few and far between.

At an intersection, Kori pulled over and Anya followed suit. "There," Kori said. "That small warehouse across the street. That's the address."

"It looks dark."

"Well, these guys are probably taking no chances. First, a remote location and, second, a dark building."

"There are no other vehicles around."

"Maybe around back. Plus, we're probably early. The note said 'tonight.' That could be anytime between now and dawn."

"I do not have a good feeling about this, my friend."

"I'm sure it'll be fine, Anya. Santiago trusts us, right? He wouldn't steer us wrong. And there's no way that Estrada's men could have gotten wind of this. C'mon, let's park our bikes behind the warehouse and look for a back entrance. Say, that reminds me," Kori said with a smirk. "Did you hear about the prostitute who couldn't spell?"

"No."

"She went to work in a warehouse."

"Very funny."

The agents rode around to the back of the building, parked their bikes in the empty lot, and found an unlocked door. Once inside, they shone their phones around until Kori spotted a battery-operated lantern and switched it on. The light was low and created eerie shadows, but it allowed them to see around the place, at least while it stayed lit. "Batteries must be loose," she said, banging on it a couple of times as the light flickered. Finally, it stayed on but Kori was careful not to move it around too suddenly.

The warehouse was vacant but for some folding chairs, a few bedrolls, a table, and a shelf of nonperishable food supplies.

"Anya, check it out. Someone could come here and stay for a day or so and be comfortable. Someone looking to keep a low profile, for instance. I think we found the San Benito west end HQ of *El Principio*."

"I think you are right, Kori. This must be a safe place for the rebels to come to when they are around here."

"Well, we might as well sit down and make ourselves comfortable. No telling when Prieto or his men might show up."

But even as she finished the sentence, the agents heard the back door opening. Someone stepped inside, pointing a flashlight in front of them, making it difficult for Kori or Anya to make out who it was.

The person stepped closer and lowered the flashlight, and in the glow of the lantern, Kori could see the figure of *El Principio* second-in-command Fernando Vallejo—a.k. a. Central Intelligence Agent Oscar Rentería.

22

—·—

"Ah, good evening, Ms. Bridges," Rentería grinned. "Welcome to our little hideout. I see you have brought a friend with you."

Kori smiled, trying not to look too taken aback. "*Sí*. Señor Vallejo, may I present one of our top foreign correspondents. This is Katalina Sergechev." Might as well stay with Russian, Kori thought. That way Anya didn't need to hide her accent.

"Hello," said Anya, reaching out and shaking Rentería's hand. "It is a pleasure to meet you, I am sure."

"It is good to see you, Señor Vallejo," Kori said, maintaining her smile. "Thank you so much for agreeing to meet with us."

"Of course."

"Will Comandante Prieto be joining us here, or are we going to go meet him somewhere?"

"Unfortunately, I am afraid that Comandante Prieto sends his regrets, señorita. He simply cannot make it. But we received word that you had something of importance to tell us, and so he sent me in his stead. I hope you're not too disappointed."

"No, no, of course not."

"Then, please, sit down. Let us be comfortable."

Everyone sat in the folding chairs, the lantern resting on a wooden stool between them dimly illuminating the circle where they were seated. Rentería turned his flashlight off and placed it on the floor.

"So tell me, Señor Vallejo," said Kori, taking out her notepad in fine journalistic fashion, "what is the latest from the rebel camp? Are you getting more people to enlist in *El Principio*?" She needed to stall. Rentería was expecting some important information. It was the reason for the meeting, after all. But what could she tell him? That Lucas Prieto's life was in danger from . . . *him*? That wouldn't exactly come as news, not to mention that it might well end up getting her and Anya both killed. Her mind raced as she tried to come up with a solid reason for having requested the meeting.

"Oh, we are doing quite well," said Rentería, politely smiling. "But let us get to the point. What news do you have for us? Then I will be happy to answer your questions."

"Certainly, of course," said Kori. She glanced over at Anya, who made the very slightest shrugging motion with her shoulders. No help there. Kori forged ahead. "Well, Señor Vallejo, it might interest you to know that, well, the information we have is, and keep in mind this comes from a top source, although the source is, and must remain, anonymous; this must be understood. I cannot emphasize that enough. I'm sure you understand. Anyway, as I was saying, it might interest you to know that the information we have, and we believe it to be true, and I think we betray no confidences in sharing it with you . . . I mean, journalistic integrity is important to us and our role is not to be biased toward any one side or involve ourselves in any way, but of course, information like this, important information, that is to say, is something we feel we have a right and a duty to share, which is why we're here tonight and, by the way, I cannot adequately convey our appreciation for your agreeing to meet with us. Especially on such short notice. It's very good of you. Wouldn't you say so, Katalina?"

"Oh, yes indeed," nodded Anya. "Very good of you. Very, very good of you."

Rentería's polite smile was gone. "Señorita Bridges," he said tersely, "get to the point. What is your information?"

"Well, sir, we, uh, have it on good authority that the US Secretary of State is getting ready to approve a weapons shipment to Estrada's army." There. That sounded plausible. Not only plausible but true, as Rentería himself knew.

"I see," Rentería said. "Well, that is very interesting indeed." Kori and Anya were both good at reading people, but Rentería's expression was inscrutable. Finally, he said, "May I ask you something, Señorita Bridges?"

"Of course."

"Who are you, really?"

Damn. That was the second time Kori had been asked that question since arriving in Miranda, the first time being in Pablo Amador's home. Had she lost her undercover talents?

"I'm sorry, Señor Vallejo? Whatever do you mean?"

"I did a little checking. It's not important how, but I happen to have some contacts in Washington DC. They've asked around. The *Washington Post* does not have a reporter named Kelly Bridges." He looked at Anya. "I suspect they do not have a reporter named Sergechev, either."

"Well," Kori chuckled, imperceptibly dropping her hand down toward her purse, which was resting on the floor beside her chair and which contained her Glock, "I'm not sure who you spoke to, but I can assure you that we are, indeed, working for the *Washington Post*. But, um, perhaps I misled you by claiming to be *directly* employed by the *Post*. For you see, we are freelance journalists. We work on assignment and are paid on a per-article basis. We are here on a specific assignment, in other words."

"Yes," Anya chimed in. "We are independent contractors. Sometimes we work on assignments for the *Post*, sometimes for other media outlets."

"Yes, indeed," said Kori. "So we're not *Post* employees per se. Katalina here has recently won an award for her independent work with the BBC, for instance."

"A story on the growth of China's navy," said Anya, with the appropriate amount of pride.

"Ah, that *was* a great story, Katalina," Kori nodded. "And quite disturbing, I must say."

"Thank you, Kelly. Yes, it was fascinating to learn—"

"Stop it," said Rentería. Then he reached behind him and pulled out a gun he'd had wedged in his belt, pointing it at Kori. "I said *who are you*? And I would ask you both to keep your hands where I can see them."

Kori and Anya both raised their hands. The Glock was now unreachable.

Was Rentería bluffing? How far could the agents push the story? If they stuck to it, would he let them go? Or would he fire the gun instead?

Kori pondered the options for a second or two and then decided on a course of action she hoped Anya would follow.

"Señor Vallejo," she pleaded, "you must believe we are who we say we are. You have seen my credentials, and you can easily find us in the online directory of the NewsGuild. Moreover—," then she stopped. "Shhh . . . listen. Who is pulling into the back parking lot?"

Vallejo looked over his shoulder for a single instant. There was not enough time to reach down and pull out the Glock, but there was just enough to kick hard at the lantern, sending the room into sudden and total darkness. Kori dove for the floor just as she heard a gunshot go whizzing past. She reached back for where her purse was, feeling for it in the blackness. She grabbed it and rolled several yards to the side. Then, keeping her head down, she scrambled for where she thought the door was, feeling along the wall for the knob, finding it, opening it, and diving outside. Anya was right behind her.

But the open door let enough moonlight in to betray their position just beyond the exit. Rentería ran toward the doorway and fired. By now, Kori had her Glock in her hand and she returned fire, something Rentería clearly did not expect. A shot went past his head and he dropped to the floor, rolling for cover behind the exterior wall. By the time he recovered and spun himself into the parking lot, Kori and Anya had made it to their mopeds. They hopped on, with Kori turning back toward the entrance where Rentería was crouched down and getting off one more shot that pierced the metal wall behind him. As the agents rode off, Rentería shot one more time, errantly sending a round over their heads. He raced for his vehicle, but by the time he made it out of the parking lot, there was no sign of which direction the agents had gone.

"Now what?" Anya asked.

The two had made it back to the city and were holed up in the abandoned clothing shop where the receiver was set up. They had rolled their mopeds inside rather than leave them on the street. Now, they were sitting cross-legged on the floor, slivers of light from a streetlamp slipping in through the boards across the front window.

"Well, we can't go back to the hotel, that's for sure," Kori replied. "That's the first place they'll look. Looks like this is going to be our home for the indefinite future."

"What do you think Rentería will do?"

"Good question. My guess is that he'll report back to Prieto that the two journalists are not journalists after all."

"And now Prieto will not trust us. Assuming we can even get to him and warn him of the pending assassination attempt, he will be even less inclined to believe us. This is not good, Kori."

"Nope, it sure isn't. The only positive thing is that Rentería doesn't know that we know about the assassination."

"Correct. He also doesn't know who we are."

"Right. He knows we're not reporters, but he must be scratching his head trying to figure out who we're with. He must suspect we're agents of some kind, but he knows we're not CIA. And I can guarantee he's never heard of Rampart."

"He also does not know which side we are on. Prieto's or Estrada's."

"Yes, that's true. He can't think that I had infiltrated the camp and found the cache of weapons as a spy for Estrada because *he's* a spy for Estrada. We'd be on the same side."

"Unless he thinks that Estrada hired a spy to spy on him."

"Maybe. He knows Estrada is paranoid. But I'm clearly an American. And a woman. It seems unlikely that a paranoid misogynist would hire someone like me to surveil Rentería. How would Estrada have even found me? Through a job-posting website?"

"True."

"And he can't think we're spying for Prieto, either. Otherwise, why would I have been interviewing him?"

"But, Kori, he might report back to Estrada about us just the same. If he concludes we are not spies for the Mirandan government, he might want to inform Estrada about us. He doesn't know who we are, but he knows we are—how do you say?—flies in the ointment. No matter what side he might think we're on, he knows we could interfere with his plans. We are in his way and he will want to do away with us."

"I'm afraid you're right. It would be great to hear first-hand what he tells Estrada. Wish the bugs still worked. Damn Cooper's got to find a way to extend the battery life of those things."

"Speaking of which, Kori, what if Estrada sweeps his office for bugs?"

"Oh, I have no doubt that he will, Anya. Probably sooner rather than later. He probably has it done routinely. Maybe once a week or so. But if he finds them, he won't know who planted them, nor what exactly was heard. Nevertheless, we need to act quickly. We still need to find a way to warn Prieto."

"It will not be easy once Rentería tells him about us."

"He'll tell Rentería and he'll tell Estrada. Like you said, we're a fly in the ointment."

"He'll convince each side we're with the other."

"And both will come looking for us."

"And, Kori, if they each think we are spying for the other side, they will not stop looking. Not until they find us."

"Yep. I'm afraid, my friend, that we're going to be pretty popular around these parts."

23

— · —

The agents munched on energy bars and continued the conversation.

"So how are we going to get to Prieto now?" Anya asked.

"I don't know," said Kori. "Even if we knew where the camp is, we couldn't get near it. Once Rentería poisons Prieto's mind about us, we'll be shot on sight."

"What if we talked to Santiago again?"

"I like that idea, except for one thing. We can't get near the hotel. Estrada's men are probably already watching the place and waiting for us to show up."

"Shot on sight, again."

"Yup."

"If there were only a way to get Prieto alone. If we only knew where he was going to be." As Anya said it aloud, it hit both agents.

"The Cathedral of the Holy Savior," they said simultaneously.

"That's right, Anya," said Kori. "We know exactly where he's going to be. The day after tomorrow. But how can we get close to him? How can we even get into the cathedral?"

"Disguises?"

"I suppose. We can go to the meeting looking like poor city dwellers."

"But, Kori, it is a secret meeting with an underground group. It is not like it is a political rally where all interested people are welcome. They are not posting flyers about it. As poor city dwellers, we would probably not have any way of even knowing the meeting was taking place. They will be watching who comes in, no?"

"You're right. And I imagine Prieto will have guards around him, too. But we need to find a way in."

"Kori, what about Luna? She said she goes to the underground meetings. We can explain to her what we are doing. Maybe we can go with her."

"Not a bad idea, Anya. But still disguised. If Rentería recognizes us, it'll be all over."

"How can we find her, Kori? We can't take the chance of hanging out in the cathedral hoping that we run into her again."

"Well, we know her name, right? Luna Segura."

"Correct. And her husband's name was Guillermo."

Kori took out her phone. "I'll call HQ and have them do a search for her home. It's about time we checked in anyway."

"What's the latest, Briggs?" Eaglethorpe said when he answered Kori's call.

"Well, Chief, we're still trying to find a way to warn Prieto about the coming assassination attempt. We had a meeting set up, but it turned out the only one in attendance was Oscar Rentería."

"Oh, crap. What did you do?"

"We stuck to our story. Two innocent journalists just trying to report on the latest political news from Miranda. And it went pretty well, too. At least until he pulled out a gun."

"Damn, Kori. Are you okay?"

"We're fine, Chief. We traded a few shots without anybody hitting anyone and Anya and I got the hell out."

"But your cover is blown."

"Sure is. He doesn't know who we are, but he sure as hell knows we're not *Washington Post* reporters."

"So what are you going to do now?"

"We think we might have a way into the underground meeting in the cathedral where Rentería is planning on having Prieto shot."

"Lay it on me."

"Well, we befriended the widow of someone picked up by Estrada's national police. She goes to the underground meetings and we believe she can help us get to Prieto. But we don't know where she lives. Can you have Cooper or Foster run a search for us?"

"Sure, what's her name?"

"Luna Segura. Her husband's name was Guillermo."

"I'll have Foster get right on it and text you her address."

"Thanks, Chief."

"Keep me informed, Kori. And do me a favor and try to stay out of any more gunfights, okay?"

"Aw, a girl's got to have her fun, Chief. There's not much else to do down here, you know."

"Agent Briggs . . ."

"Sorry, Chief. Just kidding. I'll be good, I promise."

"Thank you."

Kori chuckled and hung up.

"When we find out where Luna lives," Anya asked, "should we go straight there? I am wondering if she would be kind enough to let us stay hidden at her home until the meeting Thursday night. We cannot go back to the hotel and I do not like staying here, Kori."

"I don't either. And not just because of its lack of comforts. The fact is, it's a vacant building, ripe for vandalizing or looting. The police might even make a habit of checking on buildings like this just to make sure that squatters aren't hanging out."

"Or members of the rebel forces."

"Good point."

"And there is nowhere else to go. We cannot impose on the Amadors again."

"That's for sure. They've done enough to help us. Señor Amador has risked too much as it is. Oh, wait—there's Foster's text." Kori grabbed her phone. "Luna is in Barrio Descarado. 27 Calle Los Robles." She plugged the address into her phone. "Outskirts of town. North of here. Forty-five-minute ride on our mopeds. We'll wait until morning for rush hour and get ourselves lost in the traffic. It'll take longer, but it'll be safer. No way do we want to be traveling at night."

"Agreed. But it still leaves us with a big question: how to convince Prieto that his second-in-command is planning to kill him. Why would he believe us?"

"He won't. Not without some kind of tangible proof."

"Like what?"

Kori thought for a moment. "If we only had Rentería's CIA file. We could hand it to Prieto."

"Yes. Yes, Kori, that would work. But how to get it?"

"Well, Foster hacked into that encrypted CIA file-sharing site. Digital personnel records are probably on an even less secure site."

"Right. But even if he can retrieve Rentería's personnel file, how can he get it to us?"

"Great question. Well, why don't we ask the man himself?" Kori pulled out her phone and dialed HQ back, getting Foster on the line and explaining the situation.

"Sure," Foster said, "I can hack in. I can even download the whole file. The problem is there's no way to send it to you. Miranda uses DPI."

"Huh?"

"Deep packet inspection. It's a process that utilizes an automated program to scan emails for certain 'blacklisted' content—terms and phrases that are objectionable to the government. Can you imagine an email being sent from the US with intelligence information concerning Miranda? Ironically, it's the kind of thing that Mirandan officials would probably love to see, but the program isn't sophisticated enough to differentiate intelligence from a perceived security threat. It would read the data as possible disinformation from a foreign entity, label it as harmful or even antigovernment, and block it every time."

"Damn."

"Sorry, Kori."

"Well, listen, what if we hacked in from here? You could walk me through it."

"That wouldn't work either. You'd need internet access beyond what the government in Miranda allows. Their internet censorship is pretty severe. Just about every website but the ones the government wants its citizens to visit is blocked. All URLs are scanned and filtered."

"You're not helping, James."

"Sorry, Kori. But the only way you could hack in would be to access a government computer. And even then, it would have to be a fairly high-level government computer. A lower-level employee is probably still going to be limited on what he can or can't navigate online."

"Well, we can't risk breaking into the presidential palace again."

"Well, maybe a government office building?"

Kori's wheels were turning. "Right. How about the computer of the head of the presidential press office?"

"Sure. I imagine he'd have full internet access. Can you get to it?"

"Well, I know where his office is and I've been in the building. Listen, once we get ourselves to a computer with the access we need, how long will it take you to walk me through everything to where I can get the file and print it off?"

"Hmm . . . five minutes, I should say. No longer than that."

"Okay, sit tight. We'll be in touch."

Kori and Anya walked to the building where the presidential press office was, taking back alleys and staying out of sight. They came up to the rear of the building and crouched down behind a pair of wide, squat palm trees.

"So what's the plan?" said Anya.

"Well, there's probably a security guard or two roaming the hallways, but it shouldn't be like accessing the palace. I'll bet I can pick the lock of that back door right there."

"What are we waiting for?"

The two kept low and sprinted to the double steel doors at the back of the building. Kori pulled out her phone to throw some light on the knob. "Keyed entry single-cylinder leverset with an Avery-style lever. Pretty basic."

She dug into her pocketbook for her lockpick set and soon enough was able to turn the knob. But the door held fast.

"Damn."

"What is the problem?" asked Anya.

"Multi-point locking system. Probably a self-latching top bolt. Maybe even one at the bottom. Can only be slid open from the inside. Bastards aren't as dumb as I thought."

"What now?"

"I dunno. Window?"

"Sure. If they open. Let's take a look."

The agents crept around the side of the building, staying low and keeping their bodies close to the exterior. There was a row of windows on the first floor along the side wall.

"When I was in here," Kori muttered, "I was pawned off on a guy whose office didn't even have a window."

"Life is hard."

"Tell me about it."

"Maybe one of these offices has a computer we can use," Anya said, sizing up the windows. "We are in luck. Single-hung with simple sash locks. You do not often see windows in office buildings that open these days."

"That's because most offices have air conditioning. I'm sure this building does, too, but it looks like it was built about sixty years ago. Power outages are common so they've probably kept the windows intact so the workers can open them when they need to. Got your glass cutter?"

"Of course. Give me a boost."

Anya pressed a foot into Kori's cupped hands and drew herself up to the first window, peering between the blinds to see a darkened room with a desk and chairs. She pulled out her glass cutter, traced a circle in the glass above the lock, and then pulled the cut glass out with a small rubber suction cup. She reached in, undid the lock, and slid the window up. She squeezed herself inside then turned and offered a hand to Kori who pulled herself up and through.

"Now what?" whispered Anya, looking around the small office.

"There," Kori said, pointing to a computer on the desk. "Let's power that sucker up."

"Go ahead," said Anya. "I'll check the hallway."

Kori turned the computer on while Anya opened the door ever so slightly and peeked down the long hall.

"It's clear," she said.

"Good. I'm on, but it's password protected."

"Here, let me," said Anya, pulling a thumb drive out of her pocket. She inserted it into the USB port and seconds later was in.

"I remember that," said Kori. "The de-encryption device you used in Paris."

"Yes. But it will be no match for the CIA servers. We'll still need Foster's help. But, Kori, look. We cannot use this computer anyway. I cannot navigate beyond the home page and the user's email account."

"I figured as much," said Kori. "We need a computer with full access to the internet. That means we have to go upstairs. That's where the offices of the muckety-mucks are."

"The what?"

"The head honchos. The VIPs."

"Ah."

"Come on."

The two slid out the door and crept down the low-lit hall toward the enclosed stairwell at the end of the hallway, seeing nobody.

"If there are security guards in this building, they sure aren't very active," Kori said once they'd made it to the stairwell. But when they reached the top of the steps and she stuck her head out to peer down the second-floor hallway, she spotted two security guards idly chatting outside of one of the offices.

"Two of them," she whispered to Anya, drawing herself back into the stairwell. "About thirty feet down the hallway. They're just standing there."

"Armed?"

"Holstered pistols. Damn."

"What do you want to do?"

"I've got my Glock. I could pick 'em off before they could even draw."

"But the noise, Kori. It would bring others."

"Right. Well, I could at least hold them at gunpoint, but I was hoping we could pull this off without being seen at all."

"Yes, that would be preferable."

"We could wait a little. Maybe these guys are on rounds, meaning they'll soon be walking off to other parts of the building."

The agents sat down inside the stairwell with Kori peering around the corner every few minutes. The guards were still there ten minutes later. And twenty minutes later. Finally, after a half hour, the guards started walking down the hallway in the opposite direction. Soon enough, the hallway was empty and the agents scurried across to the nearest office only to find it locked.

"This is actually a good sign," said Kori, reaching once again for her lockpick tools. "Important people lock their office doors, right? This is probably the office of a government minister or something."

"I suppose," Anya chuckled, "but the other good sign is the actual sign on the door."

"Huh?" Kori looked up to see a nameplate adorning the door: *Jose Chavez—Minister of Health*. "Well, aren't you the observant one?"

Within two minutes, they were in, the minister's computer had been booted up, and Kori was on the phone speaking to Foster. "Okay, pal-o-mine, we have full internet access and we're waiting on you to tell us what to do next."

"Great. Okay, Kori, here's the URL you want to navigate to." Foster gave Kori the private web address for the general personnel section on the CIA's main administrative server. Three sets of user IDs and as many passwords later, Kori had entered a page where she could search alphabetically by agent name.

"Cripes, Foster, how did you get all this password information?"

"Well, interestingly it's a combination of SQL injection, cross-site scripting, and request forgery, with a little DNS spoofing thrown in."

"Yeah, I don't know what any of that means."

"It basically means we let the Agency give us the passwords without them knowing it. It's really pretty clever. You see, you start with a couple of lines of malicious JavaScript, then—"

"James, don't bother. My eyes are already glazing over. Okay, I've found Rentería's file. I'm sending the info to the printer now. Good work, Agent Foster. We'll take it from here."

"Any time, Kori."

Kori hung up and glanced over at the printer on the sideboard but nothing was happening. "Damn!" she said. "We've come this far and we can't get the file to print?! What could be wrong? Shoot, maybe the information is encrypted somehow."

Anya inspected the printer for a moment and then flipped the power button on. Immediately, the machine whirred and began printing.

"Tell me, my American friend, what do you do when I am not around?"

Kori sighed and then came around from behind the desk where she'd been sitting to collect the pages from the printer. The file was well over a hundred pages, but Kori had decided to print just the first ten, a kind of executive summary of the career, thus far, of CIA agent Oscar Rentería, complete with a headshot, a synopsis of his education and training, a condensed record of his case history, and a partial list of commendations and awards.

"That's it," she said as the last page slid into the tray. "Let me power off the computer and then let's get the heck out of here."

But as she turned back toward the computer, both agents heard the door opening behind them.

"Freeze!" came the voice of a guard and another one followed him into the office, flipping on the light switch. "Put your hands above your heads!" Both guards had their Smith & Wessons drawn and pointed. Anya slowly raised her hands and Kori followed suit, dropping the freshly printed pages onto the desk of Miranda's minister of health.

24

— · —

If two guards weren't bad enough, a third came along. Kori and Anya were not only outgunned, they were outnumbered.

"What are you doing in here, señoritas?" asked the first guard, an older man with an oval face and a bulbous nose.

"Um, we have an appointment with the minister of health," smiled Kori.

"It is the middle of the night," said the guard.

"Is it?" Kori shook her wrist and put her watch to her ear. "Stupid knockoff," she said. "You know how much I paid for this thing? Serves me right for buying a watch from a street vendor, huh?"

"Silence!" said the guard. Then, turning toward the others, he said, "Cuff them. We will turn them over to *Policia Nacional*."

"Put your hands behind your backs and turn around," one of the other two guards said as he unclipped the handcuffs from his belt. The other did the same. Both agents knew that the best chance of escape was at that moment. Anya was the first to make a move. She began turning

230

around as the guard had asked, then, when he was within reach, she spun back toward him. With a lightning-quick move, she grabbed the wrist of the hand his gun was in and punched hard at the back of his forearm. Involuntarily, his hand opened. Anya snatched the gun from him and brought it up to his head, spinning him around and taking a position behind him, still holding onto his wrist, but forcing it upward against his back and rendering him immobile.

Kori preferred a more direct assault. She, too, turned around as she'd been instructed, but then employed the position to her advantage, spinning back around and using the centrifugal force to launch a karate kick to the guard's head, her boot extending completely and making contact with the guard's chin. He never saw it coming and crumpled into a heap on the floor.

The first guard raised his weapon at Kori as she finished her flying kick but Anya's voice stopped him. "Drop your gun or I will shoot your friend here!" she said, digging the barrel of the guard's pistol into his head.

"Okay, okay," the first guard said, dropping his gun to the floor and raising his hands above his head.

"How did you know we were in here?" Kori asked, pulling out her Glock.

"Closed-circuit TV," replied the guard.

"Impossible," said Kori. "I scanned the room for cameras."

"They are secret cameras. There, the desk lamp."

Kori looked closely at the lamp and saw nothing. Then she looked even closer and saw the tiniest of cameras.

"So the occupants of these offices don't even know they're being watched," mused Kori. "I imagine the place is bugged too. So what took you so long to get here?"

The guard's expression turned sheepish. "We didn't notice right away." Then he straightened up and went on the offensive. "But you two are in deep trouble, señoritas. Deep trouble! This is an official government building. Who are you and why have you broken into this office?"

"Us?" said Kori. "We're just a couple of tourists here on vacation. Guess we got lost. And we've got a full itinerary, so if you gentlemen will be kind enough to remove yourself to that closet there, we'll be on our way. Oh, looks like you're going to have to help your buddy on the floor there. He's still unconscious. Well? What are you waiting for?"

The first guard leaned down behind his prone coworker, grabbed him under the arms, and dragged him into the closet. Anya pushed her guard in after them, and while she held her gun on the three, Kori handcuffed them with their own cuffs and then closed and locked the door.

"Let's go," she said, turning to grab the papers off the minister's desk. "There may be more. Sooner or later, these guys will be missed by somebody."

"Right behind you," said Anya.

Kori awoke to the sounds of traffic in the street outside and the sunlight making its way through the slits of the boarded-up front window. The agents had retreated to the shop, not daring to be seen on the street after leaving the government office building. Then they'd tried, with minimal success, to get some sleep on the hard floor.

Kori sat up and wondered if there was a part of her body that *wasn't* sore. "Anya," she said, standing and giving her fellow agent a light kick. "Wake up."

Anya groaned and opened her eyes. "Damn," she said, looking around. "I was hoping I had dreamed this."

"Sorry. No such luck. This is reality, sister. C'mon, we'd better get a move on."

"Is the coffee ready?"

"Very funny. Maybe we can stop somewhere along the way, but we need to be careful. Let's get out of the main part of downtown first."

As Anya stood and stretched, Kori opened the back door and peered down the alleyway. "All clear. Let's grab the bikes and *vamoose*."

The morning traffic was as heavy as the agents had hoped, allowing them to blend in with the commuters. Taxicabs were everywhere, bikes and mopeds were plentiful, and the old rambling American cars were out in full force. Kori marveled at it. For all anybody knew, the country was on the brink of revolution, the current leadership hanging by a thread, and yet people got up and went to their jobs as if nothing was wrong. At least the people who had jobs.

They took the main highway north out of the down-town area and then found a crossroad that ran toward the Descarado neighborhood. Traffic thinned and both agents kept a lookout in their handlebar mirrors for any-one who might be following. At a small coffee shop, they grabbed a couple of black coffees and continued on their way, eventually finding the barrio, then Los Robles, and then number 27.

Luna's house was like the others in the cramped barrio: small, single-story, concrete, slanted tin roof, in need of new paint. The agents rode past it very slowly, still looking in their mirrors. They circled the block once and, satis-fied that nobody had shadowed them, pulled up in front of Luna's house, laid their bikes down on the dirt, and knocked on Luna's door.

"Hola!" Luna exclaimed when she answered and saw Kori and Anya. "What a wonderful surprise! Please come in! Please." She ushered them inside and into the tiny living room. "It is so good to see you both. How did you find me? What brings you here?"

"Well," Kori said, "to be honest, we need your help, Luna."

"My help? Certainly. I will tell you anything. So long as I remain unnamed in your article, of course."

"Yes, well, about that—to be even more honest, we should tell you that we're not exactly who you think we are."

"You aren't? You are not journalists from the United States?"

"I'm afraid not."

"Please, señorita, I do not understand. Who are you then?"

"Well, it's kind of a long story," Kori replied. "Mind if we sit down?"

Luna made coffee and heard the agents out, listening with wide eyes as they described their assignment to investigate the political situation of Miranda and report back to their secret US intelligence agency. Her eyes got even wider when they told her of the assassination plot.

"Well, of course, I will help in any way I can," she said. "This is frightening news. Comandante Prieto is this country's only chance. Guillermo believed it. So do I."

"Can you get us into that meeting tomorrow?" Kori asked. "We wouldn't ask if we had any other options. You see, it's not enough that we stop the assassination. Prieto has to be made aware of whom his second-in-command really is. Otherwise, there will be more assassination attempts."

"I understand. Well, yes, I think I can get you into the meeting. Of course you will be searched at the door and probably asked some questions, but if you are with me, there should not be a problem. With Prieto himself scheduled to make an appearance, there is expected to be many people there. Perhaps a couple hundred, or even more. It is exciting to think of him coming in from the hills to meet with us. Of course you will need to dress the part. You can borrow some of my clothes."

"Gracias," said Kori.

"But approaching him and telling him of this news . . . I do not know. Will he believe you?"

"Probably not."

"How will you convince him?"

"Well, that's where you come in."

"Me?"

"You'll be able to get close to him, yes?"

"I suppose so."

"Prieto will enter the basement of the cathedral where the meeting is taking place and will no doubt spend some time before he speaks greeting people and shaking hands, correct?"

"*Sí.*"

"Anya and I will hang back. You will approach Prieto with this file." Kori handed a manila folder containing the printed pages to Luna.

"What is it?" Luna said, flipping through the folder.

"The real story of Fernando Vallejo."

"Keep it out of sight," Anya added, "until you are face to face with Prieto."

"Right," said Kori. "Then pull it out and hand it to him. With Rentería's photo on top. Then turn and get out, Luna. I imagine the revelation might start a few fireworks."

"What will you two do?" Luna asked.

"We'll be ready for those fireworks," said Kori. "Prieto will need a moment to gather himself once he absorbs the contents of the file. Then, surely he will move away from Rentería. He'll order his guards to seize him on the spot. Rentería will resist, but his attention will be on the guards and he won't see us coming. We'll come up from behind and take him down. And then arrest him on behalf of the United States government. At that point, Prieto will be pretty happy to see us and to realize who we really are. We'll tell him of the shooter on the roof of the building across the plaza and we'll skedaddle out the back door to safety."

"You make it sound so easy, taking the CIA agent down."

"Well, sure," said Kori. "After all, we'll have the element of surprise. It's a classic Agency maneuver, really. The kind of thing we've trained for a million times. It's a simple plan with a straightforward trajectory." Then Kori smiled, adding, "It'll be a piece of cake, ladies. I mean, what could possibly go wrong?"

25

—·—

"By the way, we need one more favor, Luna," said Kori. "If it's not too much trouble."

"I will do whatever I can."

"We need a place to hide out until the meeting. Would you mind terribly if we stayed here? We guarantee your safety. We can sleep on the floor tonight. We're actually getting quite good at it."

"Of course, of course. You are more than welcome to stay here as long as you want. But you will not sleep on the floor. The sofa is quite comfortable and I have a cot as well."

"That's great, Luna. We really appreciate it. Where is your son, Pedro, by the way?"

"He is at school. He will be home shortly after lunch."

"We would like to express our appreciation," said Anya. "Would you let me cook us all dinner tonight? I would be happy to prepare my grandmother's special stroganoff. If we gave you some money, would you go to the market and get us the ingredients?"

"Of course I will."

"And, Luna, get whatever you need, too," added Kori. "Courtesy of the United States government. Feel free to stock up while we're here."

"Oh, gracias, that is very kind of you," said Luna. "Things are so expensive these days. This afternoon, I will go to the market. But I will not go to my usual place. There would be some raised eyebrows if I were to buy more than my usual."

"Good thinking," said Kori. "Anya, why don't you start making out a list of what you'll need? I imagine we probably ought to add a couple of bottles of wine, too, don't you think?"

"I was thinking the same thing, my friend."

Anya's stroganoff was delicious. The women each had two servings. Pedro had three. Kori talked to him about Marco Quezada, the hero of the Mirandan National *Fútbol* Team. Anya asked him about school. "It is okay," he said. "I like math the best."

After dinner, Pedro stayed up for a little while, and then Luna sent him to bed. "Thank the nice ladies for dinner, Pedro," she told him. "And tell them goodnight."

Pedro hugged Kori and Anya. "Gracias," he said. *"Buenas noches."*

"Buenas noches," the agents smiled in return.

Pedro went off to bed and Luna said, "Let us get out of this cramped kitchen and sit in the living room."

"Can we help with the dishes?" Kori asked.

"Leave them," said Luna. "Let us open the second bottle of wine."

In the living room, Luna refilled their glasses.

"Pedro is adorable," said Kori. "You must be very proud of him."

"Yes, he is a good boy."

"And such big, beautiful brown eyes," said Anya.

"Yes, he gets those from his father. Guillermo has big brown eyes like that. Or, I guess I should say 'had,'" she added quietly.

The women were silent for a moment. Finally, Kori spoke. "I can't imagine how difficult it must be for you, Luna. And for Pedro."

"Pedro still hopes his papá is alive. Of course, I do too, but I am old enough to face the truth. Pedro is a boy. Children, of course, pick up on things more than we imagine they do. He knows Guillermo isn't coming home, I am certain. But of course he cannot admit that to himself. He continues to hold out hope. But I wonder what effect this will have on him in the long run. What will this mean for him years from now? I worry about my son."

"Of course," said Anya.

"And it is not just us," Luna added. "Many families are in mourning these days. Hundreds and hundreds."

"What is happening in your country is a tragedy, Luna," said Kori. "I wish we could do more."

"What you are doing is wonderful. It is good to know that someone from the outside world even cares about Miranda. Guillermo used to say that we are the forgotten stepchild of South America. How many Americans can even point out our country on a map? I pray every day that we might be delivered from the evil that has us in its clutches. It is hard to bear. It is especially hard here in the city. Pedro and I must begin thinking about a new start to our lives. The city is no place to be, and I fear it will be much worse here if revolution breaks out, especially if it is long and drawn out."

"Where will you go?" Kori asked.

"Back to the country. Back to my village. I am from a small village about two hours from here called Calapaya. My father has a coffee plantation. He has been sending me some money to live on. It is how we have gotten by since Guillermo's disappearance. But I know my parents are struggling, too. Everyone in this nation is struggling except for those who are in power. I cannot continue to take my father's money. I will take Pedro and we will go back to Calapaya and I will help on the plantation."

Luna looked off into the distance for a moment and smiled. "You know, as a little girl, I used to help pick the coffee beans at harvest time with my brothers. I am the youngest of five and my older siblings are all boys. I tried to keep up with them. You pick with a sack slung over your shoulder, and the more you pick, the heavier the sack gets. Sometimes it would be so heavy I could not continue! Then one of my brothers would come along and say, 'I'll carry it for you, *hermanita*.' *Hermanita*—little sister—was more my name than 'Luna' back then. Oh, those were wonderful days."

"I'm sure. Calapaya sounds nice."

"It is on Lake Isidro. The water is cool and clear. The countryside is green and hilly and beautiful. I met Guillermo there. We were happy in Calapaya, or so I thought. Eventually, though, Guillermo wanted to come here. 'There is more opportunity in San Benito,' he said. 'For what?' I asked. But I knew he wanted to get out of the village and I said okay. I liked San Benito at first. I liked the energy. The city was exciting and crime back then was not so bad. But of course that was many years ago. Things have changed so much. We should have stayed in Calapaya. This city has killed my husband, señoritas. And now I fear it will be the death of us all."

By virtue of the fact that Anya made dinner, Kori awarded her the sofa while she took the cot for herself. Both agents slept well, a consequence of having spent the bulk of the prior night on a concrete floor.

In the morning, Luna walked Pedro to school while Anya took over in the kitchen and prepared breakfast for Luna's return. Kori took the opportunity to call home. What she heard wasn't very surprising.

"Kori, I just don't know why he hasn't called," said Joan. "It's been two days."

Kori could hear the concern in her mother's voice. "When was the last you heard from him?" she asked.

"He called from the airport two days ago. Right before you and I talked. He was going to call as soon as he landed in Sacramento. But he didn't. Something must have happened to him, Kori."

"And you've tried calling him?"

"Of course. Calling and texting. Calls go to voice mail and he's not replying to my texts. I wish you were here, Kori. I wanted to call you, but I know you're very busy. Are you still in Brooklyn?"

Was that what Kori had told her mom? Yes, something about a new manager at the Brooklyn branch. Kori thought to herself that she was going to have to start keeping better notes about the fabrications she was passing along to her mother. "Yep, still in Brooklyn. We've been making some sales calls all around the city. But I should only be here a few more days."

"Well, what do you think I should do?" Joan asked. "Kori, I'm really worried about Bertram. Maybe I should call the Sacramento police."

"No, Mom, I wouldn't do that. I'm sure Bertram is fine. Maybe he just lost his cell phone or something."

"I suppose that's possible . . ." Joan's voice trailed off and Kori could tell she wasn't buying. "Kori," she said at last, "do you think . . . do you think he just took my money and . . . and . . . left?"

"Well, Mom, I mean, you know, it's hard to—"

"No," Joan said, more to convince herself than anything. "I simply won't believe that. Bertram and I had something special. I refuse to believe he could have done that to me. Besides, I'm a very good judge of character. Bertram is a good man. But, Kori, what's become of him?"

"I'll tell you what, Mom, let me call the Sacramento police for you."

"Oh, but you're so busy, dear."

"It's no problem. In fact, we have a branch in Sacramento. I'll have one of our guys there personally fill out a missing person report. How about that?"

"Oh, would you?"

"I'd be happy to. Now listen, don't ask me how I know this, but I've got a feeling everything is going to work itself out."

"Oh, I do hope you're right, Kori."

"I'm sure I am. In the meantime, try to get some rest. You sound tired."

"Yes, I didn't sleep at all last night."

"Well, get some sleep, Mom. I'll contact Sacramento and give you a call as soon as I know anything. Okay?"

"Okay, dear. I suppose I'll go lie down. Thank you, Kori. I feel much better now that we've talked."

Out of the front window, Kori saw Luna striding briskly up the walkway. Well, listen, Mom, I gotta go. I'll call you soon."

Kori hung up as Luna bounded into the house. "Señoritas," she said breathlessly, "something strange is going on."

"What is it?" asked Kori.

Anya came out from the kitchen.

"I overheard a couple of people talking at Pedro's school," Luna said. "One was asking the other if he was going to the demonstration tonight in the plaza."

"Demonstration? You mean meeting."

"No. They were very clear. 'Demonstration.' Then I left the school and the walk home takes me past an open-air market and I heard others talking about the demonstration as well. Finally, I asked someone. Señoritas, everyone from the barrios of San Benito is planning on being in the plaza tonight to protest the administration of Presidente Estrada."

"What? It was supposed to be a small, secret meeting in the basement of the cathedral."

"Yes," Anya added, "Prieto's idea was to meet with different underground groups separately. And at different times."

"These groups have come above ground," said Luna. "Word has gotten out about Prieto coming. Everyone wants to see him. An old man at the market told me he thinks many hundreds will show up. One woman told me she doesn't care if she dies tonight, as long as Estrada can see that he has lost the people. Señoritas, it was all anyone at the market was talking about. And just now, as I passed my neighbor, she stopped me to tell me to go to the plaza this evening. She is telling everyone. Word is spreading rapidly that Prieto will be there. Everyone is planning on converging on the plaza."

"The tipping point," mused Kori. "Fascinating, no?"

Anya and Luna looked at her blankly.

"It's a shift, don't you see?" Kori continued. "An organic shift in the mood and willingness of the populace. Maybe it's *the* shift. Anya, Luna, do you realize what's happening? All the pent-up hostility, all the rage, all the desperation—it's coming to a head. It's Boston on the eve of the American Revolution. It's Paris just hours before the storming of the Bastille. We've got a front-row seat to history."

"Kori, I like everything you are saying," said Anya, "but it could also be Tiananmen Square. And there was also a little something called the Boston Massacre if I remember my American history correctly."

"Yes, but Anya, there might be a difference here. This is all happening exceedingly fast. Faster than what the government can plan for. This demonstration in the plaza is going viral, which is remarkable for a country that doesn't even have social media access. People like Luna's neighbor are passing it along from house to house. And apparently, without fear. Or else maybe they just don't care anymore. They've had enough. I'll bet Prieto doesn't even know what he's riding into. How could he? Meanwhile, Estrada is walled into his palace and I'll bet he has even less of an idea of what's about to go down. Where does he get his intelligence from? The secret police and the military. But if they're gathering what we're now gathering, what do you think their response will be? Anya, we're in the intelligence game. How many times have we seen this? The generals don't have any allegiance to Estrada. Their allegiance is to power. They'll go with the flow. If they sense a point of no return, they'll dump Estrada like yesterday's trash.

They'll side with Prieto and it'll all happen just as he has envisioned."

"I don't understand," said Luna. "What are you saying exactly, Señorita Kori?"

"I'm saying hold on to your hats, ladies. There's going to be a revolution tonight."

26

"Should we start making our way into the city, Lucas?" Soon-to-be ex-CIA agent Oscar Rentería was seated across from Comandante Lucas Prieto in the same abandoned warehouse that had been the sight of his gun battle two nights before with . . . well, with whom exactly? That's what Rentería couldn't figure out.

"Yes, Fernando, the time has come," replied Prieto, rising from his chair. "How many are expected to be there tonight?"

"Maybe a hundred or so," said Rentería. "We'll take the back roads in and smuggle you into the cathedral."

Besides Rentería, Prieto would be accompanied by six guerrilla soldiers, each armed with the weapons that had arrived in the latest shipment. Rentería was especially proud of that little maneuver. Unofficially—quite unofficially—the CIA was backing Presidente Estrada. With Big Oil greasing the palm of Secretary of State Lloyd Higgins, the weapons shipments were easy enough to make happen. And since Rentería was the only person in Miranda who knew when and where the weapons were arriving, it was also easy to take control of them. They showed up on the docks in unmarked crates, and Rentería, with all the proper paperwork supplied to him by the office of Presidente Estrada, drove them off in a truck bound for the army base. Only the truck didn't go to the army base. The truck went into the hills instead.

"Okay, gentlemen, let's roll," said Prieto. A three-vehicle convoy would be taking the back roads to San Benito that evening. Two soldiers would ride in a jeep at the front, two more in the rear. Prieto would be in the middle vehicle, a pickup truck with an enclosed bed and a couple of facing bench seats. He and his second-in-command, Vallejo, would ride in the back. Two more soldiers would ride in the cab.

Upon Prieto's order, the men left the warehouse and everyone took their positions in their respective vehicles. Soon, the convoy was off.

In the darkened bed of the pickup, Prieto pulled out a bottle of rum. "Here, *mi compadre*," he said to the man he called Fernando Vallejo. "Take a swig."

Rentería took the bottle, smiled, took a healthy swallow, and thought about that delivery of weapons he'd made. That had been the key. Prieto had been thrilled—his second-in-command had certainly come through with the contacts he'd made in the ministry of internal affairs, contacts that were, Rentería had explained, sympathetic to the cause of *El Principio*. Rentería knew it was a weak story. People within the government let him abscond with crates of weapons to be delivered to the rebels just because they were "sympathetic"? But Prieto believed it because

Prieto *wanted* to believe it. Besides, what other story could Rentería tell him? That he was an American CIA agent unilaterally pushing for a coup so that he could bump off Prieto to take control of the guerrilla army, then the country, and then the oil?

That truth was, in a way, even harder to believe. Rentería felt as though he should be pinching himself to make sure he wasn't dreaming. He looked at the shadowy face of the man across from him in the truck and knew that in another couple of hours, he would be dead. "Fernando Vallejo" would be the new guerrilla leader.

"These are exciting times, no?" grinned Prieto, taking back the bottle and downing a swig himself as the truck rolled along. "It is good to be young! And we are on the cusp, *mi compadre*, of a new beginning."

"You have made it so," said Rentería.

"With your help, Fernando. And tonight, we take another step closer. Every meeting with an underground group fires up our base a little more. The momentum is shifting. It won't be long now."

No, it won't be long now, Rentería thought. *And once you are gone, the rest will fall into place.*

Rentería knew, from his CIA surveillance work and his relationship with Estrada, that the Mirandan Army was just about to break. The weapons shipments would swing the advantage ever so slightly toward the rebels. They still wouldn't have the resources of the Mirandan Army, but the Mirandan Army had gotten fat and lazy. Whatever could be said about Lucas Prieto, it had to be admitted that he had put together a skilled force of men. Small, yes, but hungry and willing and loyal. And they had learned their guerrilla tactics well. It was going to be an honor to lead them. The generals of Estrada's army wouldn't have the stomach for a long, protracted war with these insurgents from the hills.

"No, it won't be long now," Rentería agreed, smiling.

Meanwhile, the truck continued to lurch along, getting closer to San Benito by the minute.

Not only would the generals of Estrada's army not have the stomach for war, but Rentería also knew that their loyalty could easily be compromised. The ace he kept up his sleeve was his relationships with several of Estrada's officers, a perk of his CIA access to the palace. He knew firsthand that with a little prodding they would switch sides just as fast as he could offer them plum positions in his new regime.

Nevertheless, he knew that blood would have to be spilled first. Prieto was naive. There could be no "bloodless" coup. First, the guerrilla army would have to make a show of force. That was the reason behind the weapons, after all. Once established as the new leader, Rentería would order lightning assaults on governmental buildings and the palace itself. Quick hits making use of the grenade launchers and machine guns. Wipe out ten or twenty government soldiers or officials and take off back to the hills. Maybe even wipe out a few civilians. A little collateral damage wouldn't hurt the cause. A few days later, do the same thing. A few days after that, do it again. Create fear in the capital. Estrada would try to take the battle to his enemy, but his soldiers wouldn't stand a chance in the hills. It would be like sending lambs to the slaughter.

Then, Rentería would make deals with the generals and Estrada would be yanked out of his palace and his statue no doubt torn down by the good people of Miranda, the people Rentería would now be a benevolent leader to. It sure beat his day job. Twenty years in the CIA and what did he have to show for it? Squat.

"Fernando, it is not too early to be thinking about your future with my new administration," Prieto was saying in the back of the truck. "Vice president is, of course, a foregone conclusion for you."

"Gracias, Lucas."

"But I am thinking of something with even more prestige. How would you like to be my secretary of foreign affairs?"

"Secretary of foreign affairs? I would be honored, Lucas."

"Then it is settled." Prieto dug a couple of cigars out of his pocket and handed one to Rentería. "To celebrate," he said.

Rentería took the cigar and bit off the end of it. Digging into his pocket for his lighter, he thought back to when he'd joined the Agency, all idealistic and hopeful. He was going to save the world. What a crock. The Agency never gave a damn about the world. The Agency cared about the Agency. That meant making certain the funding kept coming, and that meant politics and making friends with those in power. Sometimes, it meant manufacturing a geopolitical crisis here or there so that the CIA could save the day and maintain its relevance. Hell, most of the Cold War was manufactured, truth be told. The *Us versus Them* motif played well with the American public and made the CIA irreplaceable. What the public didn't know about CIA involvement in places like Jakarta and Brazil and Chile wouldn't hurt them. They didn't need to know. And, honestly, they didn't want to know.

Rentería lit his cigar and nodded at Prieto. "Secretary of foreign affairs. Yes, indeed, I like the sound of that."

But he liked the sound of Presidente even more. Twenty years of being witness to the way the world really worked was eye-opening. There are no good guys or bad guys. There's only power. You can either own it, or you can be owned by it. For twenty years, Rentería had been owned by it. But no more. Power—real power!—was in his grasp.

"You have earned it, Fernando," smiled Prieto.

It had been so simple. Guys like Alonso Estrada were so easy to cajole. Just keep the money flowing from the States and you have them eating out of the palm of your hand. But of course there are always enemies. Rentería knew that Estrada's reign wouldn't last forever. He was far too egotistical and short-sighted. The statue in the plaza said it all. What was up with that monstrosity? Everyone in San Benito snickered at it. The problem with Estrada was that he was tone-deaf when it came to what played well with the populace and what played poorly. He was tone-deaf about a lot of things. He really believed he would hold onto his power, despite all the obvious signs. People were fed up. How could he miss that?

The growth of the opposition was inevitable. All it took was someone with intelligence and charisma to come along and lead it. Lucas Prieto was the right man at the right time. Rentería was not at all surprised that Prieto was able to build his guerrilla army into a force to be reckoned with. But if Prieto could bring about revolution, where would that leave Rentería? It was pretty well known that the CIA supported Estrada. The writing was on the wall. It wasn't just Rentería's time in Miranda—his home country, no less—that was in jeopardy. His life was, too.

If you can't beat them, join them, goes the saying. Rentería preferred another saying: If you can't beat them, *lead* them. CIA agent Oscar Rentería's life might not have been safe in Miranda, but Fernando Vallejo's life was just getting started! Soon, it would be *adios*, Oscar, and *hola*, Fernando.

"We will have much work to do, Fernando," Prieto was saying thoughtfully. He took a long drag on his cigar, lifted his head, and blew the smoke out slowly. "The entire cabinet consists of Estrada's cronies. They must all be replaced. And that is just for starters."

"We will do what needs to be done," Rentería offered.

It had been easy to infiltrate the rebel band. Rentería was a trained spy, after all. He knew all the tricks. And the story he came up with about being a disillusioned member of the ministry of internal affairs was pure gold. He could share information with Prieto that made him priceless to the movement. Becoming second-in-command had been an inevitability.

It was fun playing both sides against the middle, proba-bly the most fun Rentería had had as a CIA agent. Or ever would have. Obviously, *that* career was coming to a fast close. The office of presidente of Miranda awaited him. Oh, of course, the CIA wouldn't like it. They'd probably try to expose him for who he really was, but nobody would listen to the CIA. Rentería had it all worked out. He'd turn the country's back on the United States entirely. Make an enemy of them to the public. The Russians and Chinese had made overtures to Miranda. Maybe it was about time someone entertained those overtures. Either power would love to have a presence in South America. And they'd pay plenty.

Now, getting Prieto out of the way was all that remained. And this was the easy part. Only it wasn't going to go down exactly like he'd told Estrada. After the shooting, he'd make sure that everyone understood the shooter was a government soldier, not a member of any dissenting third faction of rebels.

The rest would fall into place. All in all, everything had gone smoothly thus far. Except for that damn *Washington Post* reporter, who obviously was *not* a *Washington Post* reporter. But then who was she? And who was the other woman? They were trained espionage agents, that much was certain. Her pulling out that gun and taking a shot was flabbergasting. Rentería hadn't seen that coming. But who did they work for? Not the CIA, that was for sure. Rentería would have known them. Were they foreign spies? The Kelly Bridges woman sure seemed American.

NSA? Nah, Rentería would have been given a heads-up. After all, he had the secretary of state in his pocket.

Of course, for years there had been those rumors of a super-secret intelligence unit. Rentería had never believed those rumors. Secrets don't stay secrets in the intelligence game. And even if those rumors were true and the women were super-secret spies, what were they doing in Miranda anyway? And whose side were they on? Other than oil, there was no reason for any kind of elite agency to be interested in Miranda. There was no reason for *anybody* to be interested in Miranda. Were they concerned about the faux nuclear program? Even if Estrada had nukes, so what? So what if he took out half of South America? Okay, Estrada was a bad man. Who cares? There is no good or bad. There's only power. What kind of power was this presumed super-secret organization after? What was *their* game?

And how much did they know? What were the women going to tell Prieto that night? Why did they want to meet with him? And whatever the message was, why wouldn't they give it to Rentería?

None of it made any sense. Rentería finally decided he wasn't going to worry about it. If they showed up again, he would tell Prieto that they were CIA secretly working for Estrada and should be shot on the spot. But why be concerned about them? They weren't going to be able to stop history. Everything was coming together. The wheels were in motion and nothing was going to stop Rentería's rise to power.

The truck slowed as the convoy entered the city limits of San Benito, then stopped altogether several blocks from the plaza.

Prieto frowned, rose from his seat in the back of the truck, and rapped on the rear window of the cab. "What is it?" he shouted. "Why are we stopped?"

The driver turned around and replied, "The people, Comandante! Look at all the people in the streets!"

Prieto's frown turned into a broad smile.

He turned toward Rentería and said, "You see? Did I not tell you it would be a good night?" He pulled the bottle of rum back out, took a swig, and handed it to the man he knew as Fernando Vallejo. "It is time for us to meet our destiny, *mi compadre*," he said. "The people are ready. To the future! To justice and righteousness. To a new beginning. For liberty, Fernando!"

27

"There must be several hundred people here already," said Kori. She and Anya and Luna had made their way into the plaza. They had spent the day trying to relax, but it hadn't been easy. All afternoon, people from the barrio, some friends of Luna's, some complete strangers, had come by spreading the word about the demonstration.

The sun was setting over the National Assembly building and the lights of the plaza had come on. Hundreds of people were milling about and more continued to stream in from the side streets. "This is amazing," Luna said, wide-eyed.

"Kori," said Anya, "where do you think Prieto will enter from?"

Kori looked over at the Cathedral of the Holy Savior. "Maybe he'll come up behind the cathedral. But remember, he probably still thinks he's headed for the basement to meet with an underground group of a couple hundred at most. He's not expecting this. Who knows where he'll go once he comes in and sees this gathering?"

"The people are coming in from all the streets around the plaza," said Luna. "He might get caught up in the traffic."

"And think about this," said Anya, "if Prieto himself doesn't expect the crowd, neither will Rentería."

"That's right, Anya," said Kori. "His plan was to usher Prieto out of the side door of the cathedral after the meeting where a sharpshooter from across the plaza on the rooftop of the National Assembly building would gun Prieto down. Now what will he do? Does he change the plan?"

"Well, if I were Rentería," Anya said thoughtfully, "I would insist that Prieto make an appearance to the crowd. Prieto will insist on that himself. Once he sees that the people are coming out to see him, risking their own welfare, he will talk to them. He will sense the importance of the moment, the 'tipping point' as you call it. Look, people continue to stream in. There are at least a thousand here now, if not more. This is Prieto's time. I imagine he will stand before his people and give the speech he was going to give in the basement, but now it will be outside to this crowd of supporters. Perhaps on the steps of the cathedral, where he can be seen by all."

"Indeed, Anya. That's the logical place. He'll rely upon the sanctuary of the church. And he'll deliver his speech from the top of the steps, as you said. Everyone will see Lucas Prieto. Including the sharpshooter." Kori looked from the steps to the roof of the Assembly building. "Cripes, you couldn't ask for an easier shot."

"But I don't understand something," said Luna. "Why would Prieto expose himself like that? He knows it would be dangerous. Why would he stand where he could so easily be gunned down?"

"Well, first of all, he knows it would be dangerous, but he doesn't know about the sharpshooter," Kori replied. "More to the point, Prieto knows that if one of Estrada's soldiers were to assassinate him, especially here in front of all these people, on the steps of the cathedral no less, mass chaos would ensue. There would be riots such that Estrada has never imagined. In Prieto's mind, it would be the height of folly for Estrada to take him down here. And normally he'd be right. But remember, Estrada and Rentería are planning on pinning the blame on another rebel faction. In front of everyone, they're going to parade some poor schmuck around as the alleged assassin and claim that the government had nothing to do with it."

"How are you going to stop the assassination, señoritas?" Luna asked, a trace of desperation in her voice.

"Good question," said Kori. "It's going to be a lot harder for us to get to Prieto now, to warn him, to hand him the file on Rentería. I mean look at this crowd. If we only knew from which direction he'll be coming from, perhaps we could stop him before he even got here."

"But there are dozens of ways to get here," said Luna. "All roads around the capital eventually lead here to the plaza."

"I'm afraid you're right. Our first sighting of him will be at the same time everyone else sees him, including the shooter."

"Kori," said Anya, "we can't stop Prieto from exposing himself to the shooter. It's impossible. We have to work on the other end of the equation."

"We have to stop the shooter," Kori said

"Yes," said Anya. "After all, we know where *he's* going to be."

"Right up there," said Kori, pointing across the plaza to the flat roof of the Assembly building. "We have to figure a way up there." Kori looked at her watch. "The meeting was supposed to start in an hour. With traffic, it's going to take Prieto longer than that to get here, so we have some time. Come on, let's go scope out the Assembly building."

The three made their way through the growing crowd. Chants and slogans were starting up here and there. "Miranda *libre*!" people were shouting. "Free Miranda!" "Long live Prieto!"

Kori looked around and was surprised by the lack of governmental presence. "Do you guys notice that there are virtually no soldiers around?"

"Yes, I noticed that," said Anya. "There were some police officers around the perimeter of the plaza before, but I don't see them now."

"Rats off a sinking ship," said Luna. "They are running scared. Look at the crowd now!"

Luna was right. By the time the women made it over to the Assembly building, the crowd had swelled to three or four thousand. The only place soldiers could be seen was inside the entry of the Assembly building. The women could see them through the glass doors. They were nervously peering out, machine guns in hand.

"Well, we can't get in there," said Kori. "Those guys look jumpy and trigger-happy. There's nothing more dangerous than a group of frightened men with guns. Let's walk around back and see if there's another way in."

The Assembly building was about three city blocks long. The women walked all around it. There were other entrances, but each was guarded by soldiers.

"They're hunkering down," said Anya. "They're staying out of the plaza, but they are making a stand at the Assembly building."

"Yep," agreed Kori. "The major symbol of the Mirandan government."

"So how do we get up to the roof?" Anya asked. "All entrances to the building are effectively sealed."

Kori looked upward. "We could climb."

"How?" said Anya, unable to hide an incredulous smile. "It is five stories, my friend. The walls are smooth."

"Well, if we had a grappling hook and some rope . . . "

"Agent Kori Briggs," Anya laughed, "I have always appreciated your enthusiasm and can-do spirit, but. . . "

"Unrealistic?"

"A bit."

"Well, what's our plan then, Anya? We have to try something. If my calculations are correct, about forty-five minutes from now *El Principio* Comandante Lucas Prieto is going to be making a speech over there on the steps of the Cathedral of the Holy Savior, a direct shot from the roof above us."

"We can work our way to the steps," replied Anya. "If that is where Prieto will go, then why don't we get there first?"

"Yeah, I guess that makes sense," Kori agreed, looking wistfully back over her shoulder at the rooftop.

"Come on, Batwoman," chuckled Anya. "We will put your superpowers to work over at the cathedral."

As the women made their way through the crowd to the cathedral, the crowd grew to more than eight thousand. It was dark now, but the lights of the plaza illuminated the throngs. The chants continued. Some in the swarming crowd were holding banners aloft: "*El Principio.*""Free the People." "Liberty."

"Kori, look!" Anya pointed to the side of the cathedral from where an entourage of six armed rebel guerrillas was marching into the plaza. Kori recognized a few of them from the camp. When they came closer, Kori could see that they surrounded two men—Lucas Prieto and Oscar Rentería. But still, the women were thirty yards away from them with hundreds of people in between.

The crowd began to close in all around the area and soon all that could be heard was the chant of "Prieto! Prieto! Prieto!" Prieto waved and smiled broadly to the crowd.

"They made it," Kori said to Anya, yelling to be heard above the din.

Anya shouted back, "Yes, and Prieto is heading to the steps just as we thought. But, Kori, we can't get anywhere near him!"

Kori turned and looked back at the Assembly building. "Anya, the shooter! He's already in place!" A lone figure on the rooftop, silhouetted by the moon above him, was holding a rifle. He lay down and out of Kori's sight. Had she binoculars, she would have seen the barrel of a high-powered rifle pointing out from the balustrade.

"Señoritas," Luna implored, "you must do something. Prieto is walking up the steps to make his speech! Oh, Prieto!"

Kori looked toward the cathedral. Then she looked back at the shooter. Then back at the cathedral. She knew it was impossible to get to Prieto in time. He was standing at the top of the steps now, waving to the crowd which was beginning to hush to hear the impassioned words of liberty that he was no doubt about to deliver. She noticed Rentería standing beside him, then, after glancing up across the plaza, he slowly moved away from him, getting himself out of the way, keeping himself safe from the shots that Kori knew would be coming in mere moments; the shots that would snuff out the life of Lucas Prieto, and with it, the life of the revolution.

28

—·—

Kori pulled out her Glock.

"Kori, what are you doing?" Anya shouted. "There is no way you can hit the shooter from here. Even if you had a clear view of him."

"I know, Anya. It's not the shooter I plan to hit." Kori looked toward the steps of the cathedral. Above the main doors were two floodlights illuminating the entryway and the top of the steps.

She shot twice.

Suddenly, the entryway area of the cathedral was bathed in darkness. Instinctively, Prieto dropped to the ground. Two more shots punctured the doors behind him, these coming from the rooftop across the plaza.

With the crowd noise, nobody heard the shots but it was clear to all that something was wrong. Soon enough, it dawned on the crowd that Prieto had been fired upon. Kori slid her Glock quickly into her purse. She and Anya and Luna slipped through the crowd, getting lost in the mass of people, knowing that surely someone had seen Kori pull out a gun. It would be easy to think she was the

265

shooter. But at the steps of the cathedral, the rebel soldiers knew better. They knew from the shots that had missed Prieto that someone was firing from across the plaza and now the gunman was standing again, no doubt trying to determine whether his shots had been successful.

"There!" one of the soldiers yelled, pointing at the roof of the Assembly building. Three rebel soldiers pulled out their machine guns and fired across the plaza at the rooftop, spraying bullets all over the balustrade. The gunman dropped down again as the rebel soldiers moved out into the plaza. The crowd gave them room and began to disperse, but Kori was stunned by the lack of panic. Nobody was stampeding. Everyone wanted to see what was going to happen. The assassination attempt had only emboldened them.

She looked back at the cathedral just in time to see a couple of the other soldiers ushering Prieto inside.

"Anya," Kori said, "Prieto has taken cover in the cathedral. And I don't see Rentería anywhere. He must be inside with him. Come on!"

The three ran up the steps which were now deserted of people, everyone having moved out into the plaza. Behind them, Kori could hear a new chant. "Storm the building! Storm the building!" The crowd had regrouped, and as Kori looked over her shoulder, it seemed as if the eight thousand people were now twenty thousand, all of them marching toward the National Assembly building.

"Luna, wait here," Kori said when they reached the doors. "I don't know what's going to go down in there. It may not be safe. Do you still have the file?"

"*Sí*, right here."

"Anya, take the file and follow me."

"Right."

Kori opened one of the two large entrance doors very slowly, knowing that armed rebel soldiers were on the other side. She and Anya stepped inside the narthex, hands raised. Prieto was standing behind two soldiers who raised their weapons. Rentería was standing to the side with another soldier. They raised their weapons, too.

Señorita Bridges!" Prieto called out. "Lower your weapons, amigos." Everyone did except Rentería. "You have come to cover the revolution! It is happening. What a story you will have! A Pulitzer for you, no doubt. Do you hear the crowd outside? They are storming the National Assembly building. I suspect they will storm the presidential palace next. I have sent word to the hills. My army will be here in mere hours. Estrada's army is no doubt running from the city. We have won! When the dust settles, before daybreak, I would think, the capital will be in our hands and the country will be ours. I will make a speech to the people."

"Comandante Prieto," Kori said, "I think the time has come for me to tell you who I really am."

"What do you mean?"

"More importantly," Kori continued, pointing over at Rentería, "I'd like to tell you who this man is."

Prieto glanced over at Rentería and noticed suddenly that he was still training his gun on Kori. "Fernando," he said. "What are you doing? Put your gun down. Señorita Bridges is a friend of ours."

"No," Rentería replied. "She is not a friend. This woman is with the government. So is the other one. They are spies for Estrada. They are the ones who tried to kill you tonight and no doubt are still planning to."

Prieto's brow furrowed and he looked at Kori with a suspicion that made Kori's blood run cold. He took a step toward her. "Is this true, señorita?" he said in a low, even voice.

"No, it's not, Comandante. It's not at all true. Your second-in-command here, the man you call Fernando Vallejo, is, in actuality, a United States CIA agent named Oscar Rentería. It was he who was behind the assassination attempt. He is attempting to gain power for himself and he intends to take control of your army."

"I do not believe you."

"Let me shoot her," Rentería said. "Let me shoot them both."

"Wait," said Anya. "Here. Comandante, look at this file. If you're still not convinced, you can shoot us then."

Prieto stepped toward Anya who handed him the file with Rentería's CIA photograph on top. Prieto turned toward Rentería. "Put your weapon down."

"No. This is all a lie."

"I will decide, Fernando. Put your weapon down."

"No." Rentería's eyes were darting back and forth between Kori, Anya, and Prieto. Kori was imagining what was going through his head. The jig was up. What would he do? He couldn't shoot Prieto because he knew the others would gun him down instantly. He could shoot Anya and Kori, though. His only hope was in silencing them both and then concocting some story that the file Prieto was holding in his hands was a file of manufactured lies. Would Prieto believe him? Either way, Kori knew that she had to say something quickly.

"Comandante, *por favor*," she said. "You cannot let him shoot us before we have the chance to explain who we are and what's in that file! Your life and the future of your revolution, indeed the future of your nation, depend on it."

Rentería raised his gun and took aim at Kori. In a flash, Prieto drew the Remington out of his holster and aimed it at Rentería's head. "Easy, amigo," he said. "I do not want to kill you. But if you pull that trigger, I swear to you that I will."

"Lucas," Rentería pleaded. "Who are you going to believe? I have been with you practically from the start. I've been your right-hand man all along. You trust me, do you not? How can you not trust me? Forget that file. Let's kill them and then get moving. Listen. Do you hear the crowd outside? They are storming the Assembly building even as we stand here. They will storm the palace next. We need to be there. We need to lead them. And then we need to prepare your speech to the people of Miranda after you are in the palace. There is much for us to do. We are wasting time!"

"I will decide if our time is being wasted," said Prieto. "I will tell you only once more. Lower your weapon or I will shoot you dead, my friend."

Rentería blinked a couple of times, sweat beading on his forehead. Kori breathed, trying to remain calm but wondering with each breath if it would be her last. She glanced over at Anya. Their eyes met and Kori knew that Anya was feeling the same.

Finally, Rentería lowered his gun. One of the other soldiers stepped over to him and swiped it out of his hands.

Kori and Anya both exhaled.

Prieto put his pistol away and then paced around the narthex, his head buried in the file, scrutinizing the information, examining the detailed record of Oscar Rentería, CIA agent. Eventually, he dropped the file on the floor and walked over to Rentería.

"You see? It is lies," Rentería repeated. "Surely you can see this, yes?" Rentería's voice was shaky, the tone one of desperation. He tried to smile as Prieto drew nearer. "Lucas. *Mi amigo*. It is me. Your loyal friend and comrade."

Kori and Anya watched then, in disbelief as Lucas Prieto, before Rentería could say another word, drew the Remington back out of his holster, put it against Rentería's head, and pulled the trigger.

29

The last anyone saw of Presidente Alonso Estrada was as he dove headfirst into a Mirandan Army helicopter that immediately took off from the roof of the presidential palace and disappeared ignominiously into the night sky. Down below, his palace was filled with the people of a city that he would never see again. The Mirandan Army was nowhere to be seen. Neither was the secret police.

Estrada would eventually be granted asylum in Uruguay where he would live out his life alone in relative squalor, his vast fortune vanishing in one magical night of revolution and rebirth in a time and country he was no longer any part of. The revolution and rebirth that he, himself, had unwittingly brought about.

The night of the revolution, Kori and Anya mingled about in the crowd, feeling the euphoria of the reborn city. Prieto had thanked them for exposing Rentería and, when his army of guerrillas finally made it into San Benito, he had been paraded by his men from the cathedral, through the plaza, and on into the presidential palace. From the balcony of the third floor, he made his grand speech to the throngs below. It was covered live on every government television network, the media having switched their allegiance the moment Estrada's helicopter took off.

Prieto spoke of liberty and freedom and of a new start for all Mirandans. He promised that the government he was going to install—including a legislative body comprised of loyal revolutionaries that would be, to nobody's raised eyebrows, handpicked by Prieto himself and including his own position as presidente—would be subject to free and fair elections within six months. "Democracy will rule in Miranda," he declared. "Our nation will become a beacon of freedom and liberty to all of Latin America!"

Fireworks went off all over the city after the speech, indeed all over the country. Prieto declared three days of celebration for Miranda, his very first act as presidente.

The morning after the revolution, with people still celebrating in the streets, Kori briefed Director Eaglethorpe on the phone from Luna's house where Kori and Anya had spent the night.

"Congratulations, Agent Briggs," Eaglethorpe said. "And pass my congratulations on to Agent Kovalev as well. Of course, when you return, we will have to discuss the small matter of your exceeding your assignment."

"Chief?"

"You were to warn Prieto about Rentería. Period. Not set a revolution in motion."

"Oh, believe me, Chief, the events of last night had a life of their own. By the time we warned Prieto, the revolution was already a lock. All we did was keep Rentería from leading it."

"Hmm. Maybe."

"Chief, I'm telling you, I've never seen anything like it. The only thing that comes close in my mind is footage I've seen of the fall of the Berlin Wall. Same kind of jubilation and revelry. Pure joy. But of course, I was only two years old when the Wall came down."

"Well, now you're making me feel old. I was there, stationed in Europe at the time. But, listen, Agent Briggs, regardless of how it went down, you must have a sense of what's going to happen next. You've met Prieto. You've spent time with him. You told me he seemed sincere. What's your gut telling you now that he's actually in power?"

"I don't know, Chief. To be honest, I saw a side of him last night that surprised me. I guess we'll know in six months. That's when he's promised democratic elections."

As the conversation wound down, Eaglethorpe wished Kori safe travels and then said, "I'm going to put Agent Cooper on now. I think he has some good news for you."

Cooper got on the line. "Kori, if you're done stabilizing the geopolitical situation in the Southern Hemisphere, I have some news for you from back home."

"Yeah? Lay it on me, Coop."

"We have him. We have Vincent Helm."

"That's great! Where is he?"

"Memphis. Ford and Baldwin tracked him down. He's got a brother there. He'd already cashed your mother's check, of course."

"Of course."

"But the good news is, he hadn't spent any of it. He had the whole thirty grand on his person. In cash."

"Whew, that's a relief."

"So, anyway, Ford and Baldwin's guys have him tied up in a motel room. They're just awaiting the go-ahead from you."

"Great. Well, you know what to do, Coop."

"Yep. Consider it done."

"And after he finishes his little performance, tell the guys to keep him there until I come for him."

"What are you going to do, Kori?"

"Do you really want to know?"

"No, I suppose not. Besides, I think I have a pretty good idea anyway."

Kori's next call was to Rampart agent Roberto Vidal to brief him on the revolution as well. Well, and also just to hear his voice. Truthfully, even with the revolution on her mind, plus her mother's situation, Kori hadn't stopped thinking about Roberto ever since the night they spent together. Turns out the feeling was mutual.

"So when are you coming to Rio again?" Roberto asked and she could sense the warm smile in his voice. An image of his toned body went through her mind. And those deep brown eyes.

"Soon," Kori said. "If you wouldn't mind a little company."

"I would not in the least mind."

"Give me a week or so to take care of some business, spend some time with my mother, and check in at HQ. Then I'm all yours."

"I like the sound of that."

"And you haven't heard anything yet."

"You're making it hard to wait. Sure you can't come sooner?"

"Just sit tight, Romeo. I'm worth the wait."

"That you are, my dear. Okay, I'll wait. But don't forget me."

"Never."

Not long after her conversation with Roberto, her phone buzzed.

"Kori, I just talked to Bertram!" came her mother's voice.

"You did?" Kori asked, trying to sound surprised. "Where is he? What did he say?"

"He's in Sacramento. He apologized for not getting back to me. It was like you'd said, Kori. He'd lost his phone."

"See?"

"Anyway, he has access to all his money again. Everything has worked out, Kori. He's overnighting a package to me with the whole thirty thousand dollars that he borrowed. I knew he was an honest man. I just knew it."

"Yep, looks like you were right, Mom." *Way to go, Coop,* she thought.

"But, Kori, here's the sad part. His sister is cleared for the kidney transplant, but it's going to be a long road to recovery. He's decided to move out there. He wants to be closer to her, anyway. She's all the family that he's got, Kori, and he doesn't feel like he should be away from her. But of course that means he can't see me anymore." Joan paused to gather herself. "I guess that means we're broken up."

"Aw, I'm sorry, Mom."

"Well, I guess it's for the best. I mean, I respect his decision to be closer to family. He's doing the right thing. Of course that makes me like him even more. But, you know, I could tell the decision wasn't easy for him. You should have heard him, dear. He sounded really upset."

I'll bet, thought Kori, and she imagined Ford and Baldwin's men hovering over him as he placed the call to Joan from his Memphis motel room and listening to him recite the script she'd requested.

Kori couldn't wait to meet him in that room face to face.

"I told him maybe we could keep in touch," Joan continued, "but he said it would be better if it were a clean break. I guess he's right, Kori. But . . . well, it's just so sad, you know? I mean, I'll never see him or talk to him again."

Kori could tell her mother was close to tears and fumbled for something to say, finally coming out with, "Well, Mom, you know what they say. Better to have loved and lost than to never have loved at all. Remember Anthony Hopkins in *Shadowlands*?"

"Not really."

"'The pain now is part of the happiness then. That's the deal.' You can be grateful for the time you got to spend with Bertram, right?"

"Yes, you're right, Kori. That's the way I should be thinking about this. He's a wonderful man and I was lucky to have met him. Thank you, Dear. I suppose I needed to hear that. It was quite a whirlwind romance and I should be grateful for it. And I do have to say that he made me feel so good about myself. He was so flattering!"

"There ya go. And who knows, there might be another Bertram out there for you. You're an attractive woman with a lot to offer."

"Yes, well, maybe."

"Listen, Mom," Kori said. "I'm flying home in a couple of days. How about I come over the day after that? We'll hang out. Maybe go to Martin's for lunch. Get our nails done. See a movie. Go to an art gallery or something. What do you think?"

"Oh, Kori, I would *love* that," her mother said, brightening. "That would mean the world to me. But won't you be tired from your trip?"

Tired? Kori knew she'd be exhausted. "Not at all, Mom. I'll be fine. See you soon!"

Kori and Anya would stay one more night in Miranda. The morning after the revolution, after Kori had talked to Eaglethorpe, Cooper, Roberto, and her mother, she and Anya said goodbye to Luna and Pedro.

"Thank you for everything, señoritas," Luna said. "Guillermo would be so happy to see what has happened. We have our country back."

"What will you do now?" Anya asked. "Stay in the city?"

"No, I do not believe so," said Luna. "I will take Pedro and I will go back home, home to Calapaya. Home to the coffee plantation. You must come visit sometime. Both of you."

"We would love to," said Kori. "It sounds beautiful."

Then the agents made their way back to Hotel San Benito. They stopped at the lobby bar to have one more beer and to say goodbye to Santiago, then they rode their mopeds to Pablo and Lidia Amador's house to thank them for everything. Of course, Lidia invited the agents in for dinner and they were happy to accept. Pablo was already healing nicely from his wounds but said that with the new direction of the country, nothing hurt anymore anyway.

Kori turned over her Glock. "Thank you for its use," she told Amador. "Let's just say it came in handy."

The next morning, it was off to the airport where Kori and Anya were taking the same flight to Rio. Anya would fly from Rio to Paris, and then from Paris to Moscow, reversing the long route that had brought her to San Benito. She still hadn't made up her mind about Nikolai. "I have twenty-two hours of flight time to think about it," she told Kori at the airport.

"I'm sure you'll do the right thing," said Kori.

"I am sure I will, too," said Anya. "I just do not know what that is."

Kori's flight would be shorter, from Rio to Memphis by way of Houston.

"And you?" said Anya. "You will do the right thing with this Vincent Helm character, no?"

"Oh, yes. You can be sure of that, my friend," Kori replied with a fiendish smile. "And then I will do it again."

30

Rampart Agent Kori Briggs had seen enough of how things worked in the intelligence world to not be completely surprised to learn, a few weeks after her return to DC from her second trip to Rio, this one unequivocally *not* for business, that CIA agent Oscar Rentería was being hailed posthumously as a hero. A courageous agent, he had, so went the story, well represented the ideals and mission of the CIA. He had helped provide intelligence that had aided Lucas Prieto in his fight for freedom for his nation, and wasn't that what the CIA was all about? He had died in the line of duty, a victim of a bullet from one of Estrada's soldiers.

She was also not surprised to learn that Secretary of State Lloyd Higgins's venality was left unpunished and, indeed, undiscovered. At least initially. He had gotten away with taking bribes and, in fact, was now changing his tune on Miranda, planning a trip to San Benito to congratulate the new president of the country. He would not be going alone, but accompanied by several representatives of the United States oil industry, including Cedric Doyle of Worldwide Petroleum and Chemical. But Cooper and Foster's sleuthing would not go to waste. Although everything they'd uncovered was circumstantial, it was enough to forward to a *real* reporter from the *Washington Post*. Director Eaglethorpe had insisted on it. The *Post* was planning on doing its own investigation and publishing the results.

Finally, six months after the revolution, Kori was not entirely surprised to hear the news from Miranda. She had told the chief that she'd seen a different side of Lucas Prieto in the cathedral that night. In truth, she had not forgotten, nor would she ever forget, the cold-blooded way in which the leader of the rebel army had shot and killed Oscar Rentería. He was not, outward appearances to the contrary, a caring, compassionate man. Prieto could be vicious. Sure, Rentería had it coming. Outside of Estrada, who deserved his fate more? But how Prieto did it, heartlessly and even casually, is what stuck with Kori. And so, although she was saddened and disappointed, she was hardly shocked to learn that Presidente Lucas Prieto had unilaterally decided to postpone the elections. "We are still in a transition period," he proclaimed. "We need steadiness and consistency at this point. This is not the time for change. But soon. Soon, we will hold free elections for the future of our glorious, democratic nation."

A year later, he said roughly the same thing. And a year after that. The following year was when the new statue went up in the plaza, in the exact same place that Alonso Estrada's statue had been. No one in San Benito could miss the tall bronze likeness of their newest, most benevolent, and heroic leader—Presidente Lucas Prieto.

Did you enjoy *Danger Level 4*?

Let others know! Please consider leaving a review on Amazon, Goodreads, BarnesandNoble.com, or wherever you purchased the book.

The Kori Briggs series of adventure spy novels by A.P. Rawls:

The Dark Tetrad

In this action-packed Kori Briggs debut novel, Kori is on the trail of a madman who has managed to steal a hundred pounds of uranium and, with the help of an equally twisted Russian scientist, is intent on detonating a nuclear bomb somewhere in the world. But when and where? Come along with Kori on this vicarious thrill ride as she follows clues from Washington, DC to New York City, Russia, Israel, and finally, Paris, the "City of Lights."

We'll Quit When We're Dead

Everyone's favorite secret agent is once again globetrotting around the world to save the day. This time she's investigating a real and imminent threat from a foreign power, a potential terrorist act on American soil so extensive that its successful deployment could well result in World War III. Follow Kori from San Francisco to Vancouver to Istanbul as she races against time to prevent a cataclysmic collision with destiny.

Danger Level 4

In this third book of the A.P. Rawls series of Kori Briggs suspense spy thrillers, Kori has landed in the middle of a South American revolution. Super-secret spy organization Rampart has intelligence that a dictator with weapons of mass destruction is about to be overthrown. But who are the revolutionaries, and are they any less dangerous? The stability of the Western Hemisphere is at stake. Follow Kori through the jungles, hills, and perilous streets of a nation on the brink of war with itself!

The Prince is Missing!

In this fourth book of the series, Kori has been tasked with the assignment of finding England's missing Prince Grayson! All signs point to a kidnapping at the hands of an American ex-con, but Kori knows there's much more to the story. Follow her and her trusty Russian sidekick Anya Kovalev as they scour the grand city of London for clues to the prince's disappearance!

Get a free gift when you register for updates at https:/ /koribriggs.com/connect/

UWS
Upper West Side Press, LLC